THE MERMAID COLLECTION

The Cost of Living

First published in 1956, Kathleen Farrell's *The Cost of Living* was her fourth novel. It is being reissued as one of Penguin Michael Joseph's Mermaids series – a collection of unjustly neglected works of popular mid-to-late-twentieth-century literature. Each Mermaid is introduced by a modern writer, reflecting on the author and book's importance to the world in which it was published and its continued relevance today.

This Mermaid is introduced by Jane Fallon, *Sunday Times* bestselling author of several novels including *Getting Rid of Matthew* and *Faking Friends*.

> To hear more about The Mermaid Collection, visit
> www.penguin.co.uk/TheMermaidCollection

The Cost of Living

KATHLEEN FARRELL

PENGUIN BOOKS

PENGUIN BOOKS

UK | USA | Canada | Ireland | Australia
India | New Zealand | South Africa

Penguin Books is part of the Penguin Random House group of companies
whose addresses can be found at global.penguinrandomhouse.com

Penguin Random House UK,
One Embassy Gardens, 8 Viaduct Gardens, London SW11 7BW

penguin.co.uk

First published by Macmillan 1956
This edition published by Penguin Books 2026
001

Copyright © Kathleen Farrell, 1956
Foreword copyright © Jane Fallon, 2026

The moral right of the author has been asserted

This book is a child of 1956 and may contain language or depictions
that some readers might find outdated today. Our general approach is
to leave the book as the author wrote it. We encourage readers to
consider the work critically and in its historical and social context

No part of this book may be used or reproduced in any manner for the
purpose of training artificial intelligence technologies or systems. In accordance
with Article 4(3) of the DSM Directive 2019/790, Penguin Random House
expressly reserves this work from the text and data mining exception

Set in 10.5/14.25pt Sabon LT Std
Typeset by Six Red Marbles UK, Thetford, Norfolk
Printed and bound in Great Britain by Clays Ltd, Elcograf S.p.A.

The authorized representative in the EEA is Penguin Random House Ireland,
Morrison Chambers, 32 Nassau Street, Dublin D02 YH68

A CIP catalogue record for this book is available from the British Library

ISBN: 978-1-405-98876-6

Penguin Random House is committed to a sustainable future
for our business, our readers and our planet. This book is made from
Forest Stewardship Council® certified paper

Foreword

'It will probably be a madly dull party,' said Alexandra ... 'There won't be the right kind of drinks, or really nice things to eat,' she warned me. 'Unfortunately – apart from us, of course – there won't be the right kind of people, either. So perhaps it won't matter.'

I said I was sure it would not matter, and what was the party *for*?

'Why, to get to know some men. The kind of men one wants to know.'

1956. The freedoms of the swinging sixties are just around the corner, but no one knows about the seismic changes to come. In retrospect, it feels like the cusp of two worlds. To thirty-something Marianne and twenty-six-year-old Alexandra, living in two small flats in the same house in North London, it's a hard slog to make ends meet as single women in a post-war world that offers independence, but still marries that with judgement and financial insecurity.

The two women have become friends of a sort, sharing drinks and confidences in the evenings. Alexandra – patching an existence as a portrait artist mainly painting cats and babies ('"Of course, it's got practically no face," she said, "just a couple of pale pink bulges, and no hair, either ..."') – decides to throw a small party inviting only eligible men. A seemingly random selection show up: a group of friends possibly all named Peter; Donald, a bus conductor with pretensions, who Alexandra has just met that day ('I don't suppose he'll come dressed as a conductor, will he? ... He'd be sure to take off his ticket thing'); Bernhardt ('a trifle odd, but very clever') who Alexandra has earmarked for a reluctant Marianne (and who, unhelpfully, brings along a female friend, Pisa) and 'fishy' mummy's boy Marius, who arrives with his actual Mummy. It's hardly the stimulating smorgasbord of beaus she was hoping for.

In a way it's a slight story, circular in plot, light on event, but the beauty of Kathleen Farrell's writing is in the observations. She has often been compared to her better-known contemporary Barbara Pym, boasting the same knack for insightful social commentary. But for me Farrell's satire is pithier. More biting. The prose crackles with wit. What I adore about contemporaneous historical fiction isn't the differences it highlights in our ways of life now compared to the past, but the similarities of the human condition. 1956 is, slightly shockingly, seventy years ago. A literal lifetime. The Korean War was just over, but Vietnam, although already begun, was still ten years away from becoming the era-defining horror that changed the world. Beyond the specific conventions of the day, however, the characters' concerns, their hopes and fears and – most satisfyingly – their humour still resonate today. Marianne is the heart of the piece, a modern heroine, self-sufficient, with no interest in meeting men (it's possible she has a sweet spot for Alexandra, although that is never more than hinted at), preoccupied with getting by, what to eat, how to afford a bottle of good wine or a ticket to the theatre on her paltry freelance typist earnings. She observes the world from a step removed but with the sarcastic bite that Farrell was known for, and which doesn't feel out of place in 2026. For example, when Pisa repeats something Marianne has told her in confidence Marianne promises herself 'never again to say anything which could be repeated, which might come full circle back to me and make trouble. Although I realised at the time that that would mean I could never open my mouth except for eating and a few general comments on the weather.'

Marianne's tendency for self-deprecating put-downs masks a deeper loneliness, though. There's a pervading melancholy in the writing, despite the sharp dialogue. A sense of a life that's over already for Marianne in her late thirties. She talks of living second-hand though other people. She harks wistfully back to her childhood: 'I dreamed myself to sleep with remembrances of a summer life in the country: the scent of grass, new-cut, and warm, soft-aired evenings; watering and clipping and planning for the future – a future which has already gone.' She's resigned to a solo old age. To being written off as she nears her forties. Thankfully that's a shocking concept for us 'older' women today. Write us off. Go on. I dare you.

Aside from Marius's flamboyant Mummy, and a passing mention of an aunt in Tunbridge Wells who Alexandra rarely sees, no one seems to have any family or a better home to go back to. No one has any support outside of the social groups they cobble together. There's an air of desperation. They're all grubbing a living, clutching onto anyone who might help elevate them both socially and financially. Switching allegiances when they get the sniff of a better offer. The women are competent, rustling up bits of work wherever it presents itself, but the men seem inadequate, adept at hiding things in an effort to couple up: Frederick – a latecomer to the group through an on/off dalliance with Pisa – his financial situation, and Alexandra's favourite Peter, his sexuality. There's a sense that none of them are quite being themselves. That they're lacking. Still, Alexandra – having met a policeman-with-potential on an evening walk – remains defiantly optimistic and upbeat, proposing another party if they can rustle up some more men: 'One almost gets to the point when anything male in shape and primeval in purpose will do excellently', she tells Marianne.

And so the conveyor belt begins again. I rather fear that if we revisited the house five years later it would still be going round in an endless loop, Alexandra's half-full glass starting to empty, Marianne's asides becoming bitter rather than amusing. I hope not. I hope they both found a way to step off and into whatever would make them happy eventually.

Jane Fallon, 2026

Contents

1. The Party   1
2. The Consequences   29
3. The Repercussions 159
4. The Cost of Living 199

I

The Party
—

'IT WILL PROBABLY BE A MADLY DULL PARTY,' SAID Alexandra.

Although this may appear irritating, it sounded charming in her soft 'lost' voice.

She was about twenty-six then; a young, appealing, ungrown-up twenty-six: short and a trifle plump, with pretty, curling fingers.

I was ten years older, which was both a grief and a relief to me.

We each had a flat in the same house; mine was on the ground floor, so-called, which was actually a semi-basement. Alexandra had an attic apartment at the top, with wonderful views and a lamentable lack of comfort. But as she confidently expected to get married soon, she decided that she would make do. In the meantime she battled on trying to earn her living as an artist, which was, apparently, near to impossible.

'I ought to try commercial art,' she said. 'Except that I don't know much about it, and I should have to get up early in the mornings.'

'You could get an alarm clock,' I suggested.

'Yes, but somehow they always go wrong, and those that don't go wrong ring very soft and civilized and blend into the background and become familiar noises. Besides, I still wouldn't know anything about commercial art, would I?'

She made just enough to exist on by doing portraits of children. She was not very well paid, and she was not very good at it.

'Besides,' as she said, 'it takes such a time before one can start. Sweets and stories and lots of cheerful bunny talk. It's rather off-putting, too. Children can be so beastly – most of them wear special pudding faces for the occasion, and of course I daren't paint them like that, so I have to make up another face, which is hardly satisfactory, and everyone's cross. The mothers are awful, too,' she added glumly. 'On the whole, worse. I don't much mind babies because they just lie and stare and stare. But then they mostly haven't got any special faces – just blobs.'

Certainly it all sounded very difficult.

She nibbled one fingernail as she pondered about the party.

'There won't be the right kind of drinks, or really nice things to eat,' she warned me. 'Unfortunately – apart from us, of course – there won't be the right kind of people, either. So perhaps it won't matter?'

I said I was sure it would not matter, and what was the party *for*?

'Why, to get to know some men. The kind of men one wants to know.' She sounded astonished.

'But you just said there wouldn't be any of the right kind,' I reminded her.

'One is always hoping that somebody not *quite* will bring along somebody who *is*.'

'And do they usually?' I asked helplessly. I had only moved into my flat a few months before, and had, up to then, no knowledge of Alexandra's parties.

'Well, they haven't so far,' she admitted. 'The only thing is to go on, doggedly.'

What would she like for the party, I asked. Sherry? A bottle of gin?

She considered this. 'I'd rather have more of something cheap. It's all a question of going further.'

We decided that I should contribute six bottles of a harsh red wine optimistically labelled Bordeaux. It cost five shillings and ninepence a bottle.

'Later on in the evening,' Alexandra was appealingly confident, 'we can pour some in a large bowl, grate lots of nutmeg over the top and add a few pints of hot water. It will be delicious.' She was silent for a minute, then added, honestly: 'Even if it isn't, they won't know by then.'

It was obviously going to be a party for the young in stomach.

'If you don't mind,' I said, 'I'll bring a bottle of grenadine, too. Just in case. It will look more or less the same red, and no one will notice.'

'Oh, and you won't forget, Marianne darling, if you meet anyone interesting between now and then, to bring him along?'

I promised that I would not forget. Although it seemed unlikely that I should meet anyone interesting.

Life being expensively difficult, I was trying to augment my small income by typing other people's manuscripts. Mostly they were sent by post, and those who insisted on bringing them personally were usually either self-preoccupied adolescents or middle-aged, fretful 'researchers' who had left work over until the last minute, and who were resentful at having to waste money on getting their stuff typed.

'Anyone nice today?' Alexandra always asked the same question as she came to drink a glass of sherry with me at about six o'clock.

'No one at all. A thesis on ceramics in practically illegible handwriting arrived by special messenger this afternoon. Some of it seems to be in Chinese. And fifty different knitting patterns for a mothers' circle. Both required urgently. What a hope.'

'No one *new* for tomorrow night?'

I shook my head. The question was becoming tedious.

'What about you?' I asked, obediently.

'A moderately well-behaved child, nine-ish, with lovely red hair, and no nose to speak of – twelve guineas – and it will take me days and days.'

Her light-brown hair feathered pleasantly around her ears; a smudge of charcoal shadowed one cheek; she looked tired.

'Oils?' I asked.

'No, pastels. I seem to get in such a mess, though.' From the large patch pocket of her jeans – her 'working' clothes – she drew out a hand mirror and a handkerchief. She regarded her reflection with some distaste and wiped the black from her cheek.

'I think,' she said, 'I look just a bit like Charlotte Brontë. But less intelligent.'

'And much prettier,' I said encouragingly.

'Oh, I do hope so, but often I feel that it might be better just to look intelligent. As you do. There's an awful lot of prettiness around, and it doesn't actually get one anywhere.'

'Neither does looking intelligent,' I said sourly. 'At least it hasn't me – so far – and I've been looking it for a good many years, now.'

'Darling, I know.' She leaned forward and kissed me lightly. 'It's ghastly how we waste ourselves. But I have got hold of someone who may be up your street – if only you can relax a bit. I mean, don't be *too* stiff all the time. It's so unnecessary. His name's Bernhardt, and you simply mustn't be put off at first –'

'That sounds ominous. I suppose he's just about the ugliest and most unprepossessing man anyone's ever seen, and it's up to me to discover that he has a heart of gold.'

Alexandra pouted slightly. 'Not exactly. He does look a trifle odd, but he's very clever. Something to do with statistics, I believe.'

'He sounds fascinating,' I said coldly.

'It's no good being proud. Even a few decent dinners and a theatre now and again might bolster one up no end. After all, the chief thing is to know as many men as possible, and then they'll bring along their brothers and their friends, and one *might* come across just the person.'

'Anyone of my age, or more, who isn't married, probably *is* odd, as well as looking odd.'

It was useless to explain to Alexandra that I had long ago decided that I did not particularly wish to get married, and that I would just as soon remain in a state of spinsterish discomfort as scheme to embark upon another state which might turn out to be just as uncomfortable, with the added disadvantages of being unfamiliar. She would not have believed me, and it would, too, have appeared churlish, particularly when she was trying so hard.

Alexandra was reproachful. 'You're always so cynical. It doesn't do. It makes men feel inferior.'

'Quite a few of them are,' I reminded her.

Alexandra sighed, and accepted a second glass of sherry. She seldom had more than one glass.

'What's the matter?' I asked.

'Well, coming back from shopping today, suddenly the basket got heavier and heavier, and it was drizzling a bit, too, so I decided to take a bus – and what do you think? The conductor tried to make a date with me, and it knocked me back, because I thought if *that's* what I look like ... and when I came in I stood in front of the hall mirror – the cruel one – and saw myself as if I wasn't myself, I realized that that's what I did look like – only worse. It must be the gaudy mackintosh. That certainly was a mistake. And as I looked and looked a dreadful dreariness came over me. I almost began to be thankful about the conductor – terribly grateful that he'd thought it worth trying.'

'And was he a nice conductor, as conductors go?'

'Actually quite a pet. Young and rather good-looking. His name's Donald. As a matter of fact he's coming tomorrow night.' She was silent for a few seconds, and then asked, anxiously: 'I don't suppose he'll come dressed as a conductor, will he? He must have some other clothes.'

'Unless he hasn't time to go and change,' I teased her.

She was momentarily appalled. Then she pulled herself together. 'People might think it a joke – and anyway he'd be sure to take off his ticket thing, so it might seem like a uniform of a peculiar sect. Or wouldn't it?'

'It wouldn't,' I said firmly. Then I relented. 'I expect he'll be just that added touch of the unexpected which every party is supposed to need.'

She smiled; happy again.

When she had gone I drove myself to make a start on the ceramics. After all it wasn't in Chinese.

Privately I thought that Donald, the bus conductor, would probably be better company than the statistician, who had evidently been wished upon me. Alas, Donald was far too young. It becomes more and more difficult to remember how old I am, and especially to remember that I get older year by year. Age begins to be viewed as a misfortune thrust upon other people; an affliction which one might, with luck, escape. Only when, for instance, I look at my driving licence, and realize that I have had one for nearly twenty years, does the truth overwhelm me. I am, quite definitely, getting old, and getting old as progressively, and relentlessly, as everyone else.

The next day I pounded away at the ceramics, and Alexandra tortured herself trying to get the right shade of red hair in pastels (which, having seen the result, may have been within human power, but was certainly not within hers), and we decided to 'get ourselves ready' first, and afterwards I would help her with the preparations for the party.

Everything was arranged by a quarter to eight, and from eight o'clock onwards the guests were expected.

'I won't try to tell you about everyone,' said Alexandra. 'It will be such fun for you to find out. But there's one thing I will tell you: Marius is going to bring someone very, very special.'

I made appropriate sounds of pleasure and mystification.

Marius I had already encountered. He had a way of precise enunciation, curly black hair, and one of the largest signet rings in the world. There was something fishy about Marius. I think he even felt so himself. He was always trying to put himself in a good light, and making his background clear. The harder he tried the more murky it became.

'Dear little Alex and I met most fortuitously on the Backs,' he told me, confidentially. 'She helped me to get my pole up. I was never really at home in a punt.'

Whether he intended to convey that he and Alexandra were both 'up' together, or whether they had merely both happened to go punting around the Backs to no purpose, I never found out. It is better not to know too much. One becomes responsible.

If Marius had indeed been 'up', he had allowed himself to go disproportionately down since. He was, as far as I could make out, employed by some large firm of publishers as a 'ghost' writer. He seemed to sit around in their offices, day in and day out, waiting to be called upon to rewrite memoirs of famous (but not very famous) men, or illiterately phrased stories of escapes, and turgid descriptions of dangerous expeditions. A wretched pond-like life, into which he had sunk, leaving little trace. Yes, there was something decidedly fishy about Marius.

'I shall look forward to seeing what Marius can produce,' I said.

'I know you don't care for him, darling, but he's awfully reliable, and I feel that I can talk to him – by the hour.'

I felt near to being sorry for Marius then.

The first arrivals were a group of undistinguished and indistinguishable young men, all, as far as I could make out, called Peter. It wasn't possible. Yet, wasn't it? They all sat in a further corner and began to twitter cheerfully among themselves.

'The Peter over there – that one in the middle – is my special fancy, and the others seem to go with him,' Alexandra explained anxiously. 'My Peter – yes, that one standing up now – is really awfully nice, but a bit vague. He said he'd try to bring along a friend of his who has a brother who is married, and he, the brother, might commission me to do a portrait of his child. I don't know yet which one is the brother.'

'Perhaps they all are?'

Alexandra looked sideways at me. 'I shouldn't think so, would you? I expect I'll find out.' Then, feeling that she had to protect all the Peters from the least likelihood of my disapproval, she added: 'Poor pets, I expect they're nervous, and they'll warm up later, and be more forthcoming.'

All the Peters were laughing cosily, obviously at some very private joke. They weren't noisy about it; just happily banded against the world outside. They seemed to lack the social spirit.

'When the others arrive,' said Alexandra hopefully, 'we'll be able to break them up.'

I doubted it, but I did not want to disillusion her.

Next came Bernhardt. I felt that I should have known him anywhere. He was short and square, wearing very thick spectacles; he had a sharp pointed nose which suddenly turned sideways at the tip in a most disconcerting way. His hair was brown and white speckled. He looked worried.

Alexandra greeted him joyously: he kissed her hand and began to speak urgently, quickly, in Middle-European accents. Afterwards I found that he could speak English perfectly well – he only forgot how to speak when he was nervous or upset. Alexandra kept on interrupting him, playfully pushing him towards me. She was determined to make him understand what was required of him.

'This is my dearest friend, Marianne,' said Alexandra. 'You'll like her enormously, and I've been longing for you to meet.'

Bernhardt took my hand absent-mindedly, held it as though it were a pig's trotter which he had not made up his mind whether he would buy, then, sighing noisily, kissed my fingers three times – damp, cold little pushes – after which he dropped my hand unceremoniously, and started once again to mutter urgently to Alexandra.

'It is this,' he said. 'I have very nice girl, very lonely, so I think to myself, I will telephone and ask to bring along. But telephone does not work, as telephones never work.' He was sweating profusely, and I nodded kindly at him, feeling his distress as my own. 'So I press button, bot nothing happen. No pennies come back. So there I am with nice girl and very lonely at end of road outside, and telephone don't work. So as you are kind, and it is very nice girl, I think . . .' He took out his handkerchief and mopped his forehead.

Alexandra looked bewildered. The momentous meeting between Bernhardt and myself was obviously out of hand, and nothing was what she had expected.

'So you brought her along?' I asked, unable either to suffer myself or to see such suffering any longer.

A lot of creases in Bernhardt's forehead suddenly uncreased. He looked quite smooth and human again.

'So I brung her,' he said gratefully. 'I mean I brought her. That is all right?'

Alexandra allowed her fury to take over her face for a few seconds, then, gracefully, she gave in, and smiled. 'Well, where is she, then?' Alexandra asked.

'I leave her at the bottom of the stairs,' said Bernhardt. 'I go and fetch, yes?'

'Yes, of course.' Alexandra was impatient. 'Letting her wander around in the dark all by herself. How absurd you are, Bernhardt. Why didn't you bring her up with you?'

'I bring myself,' said a small clear voice. There was silence while we all turned to stare at the doorway. There stood the girl, very slim, very young, and extremely pretty. She was dressed in scarlet silk which was complicatedly draped and swathed around her. Her long black hair was knotted back and plaited with scarlet ribbon. The effect was bizarre, and rather too attractive for Alexandra's liking – or for mine. The girl came demurely forward, and made charming obeisance to Alexandra; a half bow, half curtsey.

'I am Pisa,' she said composedly. 'It is very good of you to allow me to come to your lovely party.'

Bernhardt listened intently as one might to a child who has been taught to say her piece. As soon as Pisa had spoken her last word, Bernhardt was ready.

'That is enough,' he said sharply, giving her a quick ungentle push on the shoulder which sent her hurtling on to the sofa. 'You sit down now and keep quiet. You enjoy party. Alexandra and I have much to talk about.'

He turned his back on Pisa and drew Alexandra away. He was obviously a masterful type.

Pisa, in no way put out, gathered herself up, rearranged the swathes of her skirt, drew the heavy knot of beribboned hair from the nape of her neck and placed it curvingly over one shoulder, crossed her ankles, and looked up at me with a shining smile.

'Now we will talk,' she said beguilingly. 'You come and sit down by me, and we get to know each other?'

Weakly, I nodded, and sat down. Obviously she, too, was masterful in her own way.

Pisa leaned towards me, and said, 'Excuse?' as she picked up a fold of my dress.

'Very good material,' she said. 'Very rich. It will last long. How much a yard?'

I said I didn't know. I hadn't bought it by the yard.

'You buy ready made?' Pisa stared sadly at me. I had disappointed her. 'Very dear way of buying. Now this stuff, here' – complacently she patted the scarlet silk – 'I buy in sale. Very cheap, very cheap indeed. Three yards at fourteen shillings and ninepence, and a bit over, which they give free – the end of a piece, you say. I make it up in half an hour. Is all pinned underneath.' She lifted up her skirt to reveal lines of tacking stitches interspersed with several nappy-sized safety-pins.

Bernhardt made a little rush at her. 'Naughty!' he said, smacking her briskly on the arm. 'Pisa must behave in England.'

Pisa yearned upwards at him, then rolled her large dark eyes towards the Peters who were still laughing and chatting happily in their corner and who took no notice.

'Very fonny men in England,' Pisa said. 'Very fonny indeed.' With which I felt I could wholeheartedly agree. 'In any other country,' said Pisa, unfolding her hands, and then carefully folding them up again and replacing them in a neat little heap in her lap, 'we would think things if men played together in that fonny way.'

'Sometimes we do think things,' I replied unguardedly.

'You do?' Pisa gleamed expectantly. 'Tell me what sort of things.'

'Not just now,' I said hurriedly.

'You give me your address,' said Pisa, 'and we meet for coffee and cakes, and then we talk and talk.'

I agreed. Life began to be more and more complex: what with bills unpaid, and people, and parties, and Bernhardt, and Alexandra, and a couple of brace of Peters, and the knitting patterns not yet begun – and now Pisa. I could envisage hours of precious, moneymaking time dripping away on tinkling talk about how 'fonny' Englishmen were.

'You know why I am called Pisa?' she asked.

I shook my head.

'Because that is where I was born. Just leaning against the tower. Not me, but my mother. It surprise my mother very much.'

'I'm sure it did.'

Bernhardt made another of his sudden rushes. 'She is not Italian at all,' he said sternly, sitting down on the arm of the sofa next to Pisa, digging his elbow in her neck, and leaning heavily upon her. 'She likes to pretend she is. Her mother was half Italian, and her father, no one knows. Maybe Hungarian, maybe not. She is all nationalities.' After his first panic his command of English had returned.

'And who cares?' Pisa asked with good-tempered unconcern, after which she wriggled herself free and swayed across the room to join the Peters. One of them brought her a footstool and she settled herself down in the middle of the group, from which came little flurries of laughter.

'Well,' said Alexandra in significant tones, sidling up to me. 'What do you think of that?'

'She's rather overwhelming,' I said, 'but I must admit she's a definite addition, especially all that flame-coloured silk.'

Glowering like two disgruntled hawks, we watched her.

'Bust thirty-five, waist twenty-three, if that, hips thirty-five, height about five feet six, would you say?' Alexandra asked in an awed voice.

'Just about,' I said. 'It really is sinful, isn't it? Fancy being like that absolutely naturally. And I bet she eats like a horse, and probably never takes any exercise.'

Bernhardt, who had wandered away, came back carrying two glasses of gin and something, which tasted peculiar, but reviving. He had brought the gin, which was nice of him, although the least, perhaps, that he could do, having also brought Pisa, who, alas, did not even need gin.

'Very bedworthy, no?' Bernhardt asked somewhat thickly, watching the scarlet silk shape with myopic but lascivious interest.

'I wouldn't have put it quite like that,' said Alexandra. 'But now you mention it, the answer is Yes, definitely.'

'And is she?' I asked.

Bernhardt looked hard at me. 'I don't know,' he said.

'No,' I said. 'I thought you didn't.'

Alexandra looked from me to Bernhardt, then across to Pisa, and to the Peters, then she looked at her wristwatch.

'Where's Donald, the conductor, and Marius, and whoever Marius is bringing with him?' she said. 'If they don't hurry up there won't be anything left to drink.'

'Perhaps you'd like me to get cracking on the Bordeaux mixture, would you?' I asked.

'Let's wait a little. We may be able to drink it decently, neat. They may bring something. I mean Marius may – not the conductor.'

'I have two tickets for the Schubert in the Town Hall next Wednesday,' said Bernhardt, turning towards me. 'Would you like to come?' Then he added, truthfully: 'As Pisa can't.'

'Not that kind of conductor,' Alexandra interrupted. 'A real one, on a bus.'

'So?' Bernhardt sounded bemused.

'I'm sorry,' I said, 'but I've got lots of work to do, and I shall still be terribly busy next Wednesday. In fact I ought to be busy for the next dozen or so Wednesdays, and all the other days, if I'm ever going to get through.' Bernhardt looked sad and cast down. 'Perhaps,' I suggested, 'Pisa has a friend?'

Bernhardt laughed harshly. 'She has many men friends, but women she does not like so well.'

'I really don't wonder why she won't come with you, Bernhardt,' said Alexandra. 'I should think she's black and blue where it doesn't show. All that pushing about. I didn't know *that* was what you liked to do.'

'Not to Englishwomen,' he said simply. 'These foreigners expect it. They are different from you.' With a bow he departed and went over to Pisa, and realizing that we were both watching he decided to show us, forcefully and immediately, the correctness of his statement. He gave Pisa a resounding smack on the bottom. She jumped up with little chirruping cries of joy.

'Obviously,' said Alexandra, 'they are different from us.'

We took advantage of Bernhardt's temporary absence to help ourselves to another gin each. After which we felt better. They all seemed to be eating and drinking whatever was around, and everyone sounded gay. They were all talking at once, which was a good sign.

At that moment Donald entered. His ordinary nice-looking face was blurred by an expression of constant sympathy. One felt that he was ready to say 'there, there' and to listen to all one's troubles.

Desultorily Alexandra took him around and began to introduce him. Donald seemed to take to me; maybe he thought I was the confiding type. It wasn't that he was emotional; just naturally helpful. He had brought a quart of beer and twenty Player's. Both of which Alexandra received with sincere expressions of gratitude.

He sat down beside me and smiled. He had a really pleasant face, if only he could have stopped himself being so genuinely interested in other people, which, if carried to excess, can become tiresome.

'I oughtn't to be here at all,' he said. 'But I felt I couldn't miss the chance, even though it did mean cutting evening school.'

'What are you learning? I mean studying?' I asked.

'Shorthand and typewriting.'

'Why? Don't you like conducting? I mean conductoring?' The gin was taking its toll.

'It's a bit draughty,' he said cheerfully. 'And, besides, it doesn't seem to get you anywhere, except to Peckham Rye and back, and I've been on that damned route – begging your pardon – as long as I can remember. Enough to make you want another war. Now the clerks work inside, and there's room for advancement, if you're willing to wait.'

One of the lesser Peters from the edge of the group had made his way, crabwise, towards us. 'So you're going to be a clerk, are you? A general transport or a confidential one?' The lesser Peter eyed Donald's clothes with contempt.

'Just general,' Donald replied quietly. 'I can't aspire to the confidential, yet.' Then turning towards me he said: 'Not one of Eliot's best, do you think?'

I began to like Donald, and we settled down to a comfortable chat about shorthand and typing. He was disturbed when he discovered that I did not know at what speed I could type, although I spent most of the day typing.

'But you see,' I explained, 'there's always the laundry, or the milk, or the window cleaner, or shopping, and one never gets a clear run, as it were.'

Donald frowned. 'You ought to take an office, and make yourself into a limited company,' he suggested at last.

'Good heavens, no. Then I'd have to pay an accountant to look after the company, and there'd be rent for an office, and heating, and everything. I'd never make enough to pay the bills, let alone keep myself.'

'You don't look as though you eat enough now,' he said, letting his sympathy overrun his face.

'I don't want to get any fatter. It isn't fashionable. Besides, I'd have to buy new clothes, and I couldn't afford that. And you needn't tell me that I could alter the ones I've got, because I couldn't. I'm not that kind of woman.'

Donald patted my hand and made soothing cluckings of understanding, which, allied to the gin, nearly brought tears to my eyes. I began to feel that Donald had set himself out to be a softening influence, and I was in no position to be softened. Frankly, I just could not afford that, either.

Somewhat to my guilty astonishment, I heard myself accepting Donald's invitation to accompany him to the Schubert recital at the Town Hall next Wednesday. Bernhardt heard it, too, and fixed me with a look of complete and humiliating comprehension.

'Zo,' said Bernhardt, lapsing into an unnatural guttural which he must have kept by him for such moments, 'you vill go with a bus, but not with me? And I was told that Englishwomen are always so courteous to the stranger in their midst.'

'Don't take any notice,' said Donald well-meaningly. 'He's drunk.'

Bernhardt swung himself around with an almost military movement and stalked away. He was evidently offended.

'He's not drunk,' I said. 'But perhaps I am.'

'Women,' said Donald firmly, 'do not get drunk.'

I staggered off to breathe the blessedly cool air outside the smoke-filled room and I hoped, fervently, that Donald was right. Surely he must be right? Women do not get drunk.

I came back just in time for the great commotion. Marius burst into the room, looking strange and rare. His hair curled rather more than necessary; his waistcoat was embroidered with stars and fishes.

'Alex, my love,' he syruped, oozing towards her, and taking hold of both her hands, 'I salute you, most adorable of women. Have I ever told you that your hands are just perfect? And I mean it, I wouldn't deceive you . . .' He stared raptly at her hands and gasped a little – perhaps from the effort of convincing her. 'And I have brought my wonderful surprise –'

Alexandra, a trifle wilted by this time, but ever hopeful, managed to look starry-eyed and ready for the best of all possible surprises.

'Here,' said Marius with many flourishes, 'is Mummy!'

Mummy was an absolute riot. She had crisp auburn hair greenish at the ends, and a long cigarette holder. She was draped in banana-coloured lace, and around her shoulders was wound a strip of tiger skin; the spare end of the tiger she carried over one arm.

Mummy was what the Peters had waited for all their lives. They clustered around her with twitters of admiration.

Mummy was a short plumpish woman with beautiful legs and very slim ankles. She had a creamy skin and a creamy voice; she was elegant with the elegance of a woman past middle age who has nothing to lose, having lost everything long ago.

'Do you think,' I asked Alexandra when the room had begun to settle down again, 'that we shall grow old like

Mummy? It would certainly be something to look forward to, wouldn't it?'

Mummy's carefully musical laughter rose above the conflicting voices.

'No,' Alexandra was regretful. 'I don't think we shall grow old at all like Mummy. I think we shall just grow old, and that will be that.'

It was a pity, but I had to agree with her.

All the Peters were still captivated.

I nodded towards them. 'They feel safe with her,' I said. 'That's why they can't tear themselves away.'

'Let us hope,' said Alexandra, with a positively devilish smile of which I had hitherto not thought her capable, 'that she feels safe with them. And serve her right.'

'She certainly must have been something,' I said. 'I wonder what it was like, being sought after, and receiving flowers, and valentines, and *poissons d'avril*. I had one of those once, but somehow I never really trusted it. Not quite.'

'That's the worst of it all, for us.' Alexandra kindly included herself in my generation. 'We don't trust, do we? Nothing means what it seems to. We have to guess, and exhaust ourselves with hints and innuendoes, and often we jump the wrong way, or we don't jump when we ought to. I think things must have been very very easy for Mummy. She looks all sleek and sure, doesn't she?'

'Yes, she does,' I said. 'But no doubt,' I added comfortingly, 'we must have plenty of compensations.' I was glad that Alexandra did not ask what, because at that moment I could not think of any.

Donald backed towards us. He had been listening, stupefied, to Mummy.

'What a noise that woman makes,' he murmured.

'Oh, Donald, I do like you.' I could not resist thanking him.

Donald retreated a little, and then, seeing that my intentions were strictly impersonal, relaxed and sat down by my side.

'Don't worry,' Alexandra reassured him. 'Mummy has been rather too much for us.'

'Am I staying too long?' Donald asked.

'No. Please, please stay,' Alexandra begged him. 'You're so real.'

Donald regarded his hand, which held a glass, as if he suddenly had doubts. 'Yes,' he said at last, 'I suppose I am.'

But he wasn't very happy about the trend of the conversation, and soon he rose, gave us a self-conscious little smile, and ambled over to join Marius, who stood alone, surveying Mummy's havoc with pardonable pride. Then Donald and Marius became contentedly immersed in one of those thoroughly lowering discussions which occur some time at every party; a discussion which accepts the inevitability of the hydrogen bomb and the immediate destruction of everything and everyone. Half sober, one catches a few phrases here and there; so that is that, one thinks; all is so bad that one hardly needs to worry; life and love and accounts, paid and unpaid, and the past, and the present, and the foolish schemes for the future, will all be gone; all gone into the same large grey hole, all razed to the ground, if any ground is left for anything to be razed to. Donald, perhaps more distressingly, did not believe in total destruction. From what I could gather he favoured the view that part of the world would be blown up, but not necessarily us, and that we should be left to struggle on in a parched, soilless desert, bereft of hope, bereft of practically all, except the glimmerings of life itself. We should have nothing left except the memory of obligations which we could not fulfil, and desires which we could not assuage.

Donald, far from being a comforter, was obviously a realist in a big bleak way.

One of the Peters was playing the piano; some kind of sambo or mambo; Mummy, regardless, was dancing the Charleston. She certainly had remarkably beautiful legs, and I wondered whether she spent hours with her legs straight in the air, holding in her stomach muscles, or whatever one is advised to do. I decided that she just had beautiful legs, which nothing and no one could take from her. Only death. It was almost a consolation to envisage the possibility of my having perhaps twenty years of walking about on most ungainly legs, while Mummy and her slim, slim ankles decomposed. Then I was ashamed of myself, and I decided never, never to drink gin again.

'Marius, sweetie,' Mummy trilled. 'Have you forgotten our little present?' She was out of breath, I was pleased to hear.

Marius beamed and produced a bottle of brandy. A whole bottle, and good brandy at that.

We all thanked Mummy and Marius, and then there weren't enough glasses, so all the Peters toasted Mummy out of cups.

By that time Marius had evidently decided that Mummy was well and truly launched, and he could let himself go wherever his fancy willed. Oddly enough, his fancy turned towards Pisa, who, as he told the assembled company, was a 'thoroughly natural unspoiled sort of gairl'.

Alexandra drank off the rest of her brandy in furious haste, and said: 'There goes my once-a-week evening out, if I don't look slippy', and with praiseworthy firmness she detached Pisa from Marius's laxly encircling arm and drew him into the corner of the room, where she worked upon him with painstaking sweetness.

'Pisa come and talk to you,' said Pisa sickeningly, throwing herself temptingly down by my side.

'That's right,' I said. 'You come and talk to me, and leave the gentlemen alone.'

Pisa opened her eyes very widely with an innocent, new-born gaze, then winked at me with deliberation.

'Pisa feel very quiffy,' she giggled. 'Very gay. What about we all go out and walk for hours and hours, and watch the sunrise?'

'Not at my age,' I said firmly. 'I wouldn't wear well enough. Neither would Mummy. And although Marius might agree, he'd never forgive you afterwards. He doesn't look in good shape for dawn-watching to me. Alexandra's got to work tomorrow, and so has Donald. You might try one of those over there.' I nodded towards the Peters.

Pisa wrinkled her nose.

'Or what about Bernhardt?' I had almost forgotten that Bernhardt had brought her.

'Ach, Bernhardt,' she said expressively. 'It would be like listening to the lark with a professor of gymnastics.'

I saw her point.

Mummy was already wilting fast. She had rather over-played herself.

The Peters had been somewhat broken up by Mummy's big Charleston scene, and had not managed to get themselves organized again.

Marius had attached himself to Bernhardt now, and Alexandra had secured the tallest, most presentable Peter, the central one of the group, for herself. They were both drinking brandy out of the same cracked cup.

What a time, I thought, it has taken her to get around to what she wanted. Poor child.

Suddenly Bernhardt, having dealt with every aspect of market research, and having succeeded in convincing Marius either for or against, I could not discover which, made a sudden lunge for the door, and said that he must go. He had already said goodbye several times before, but had made no move to follow up.

'You're taking Pisa, aren't you?' I called after him.

Obviously she had gone clean out of his mind.

'She live just at corner. She is having lovely party, aren't you, Pisa? I leave her.' He spoke with finality.

'Lovely party,' crooned Pisa. 'Pisa very, very happy.'

'But Bernhardt –' I began. He had gone.

Mummy was looking quite raddled, and her hair resembled seaweed. Mummy ought to have been in bed a long while ago.

'Marius,' I implored, 'will you be a dear and drop Pisa when you and Mummy go home?'

Marius smiled benevolently and said something in Latin which I could not understand. He rolled his eyes suggestively at Pisa. It was a pity he wore pince-nez, but perhaps he was one of the *avant-garde* and they were coming in again.

I doubt whether Pisa understood Latin either, certainly not as pronounced by Marius, with much stressing of the sounds of k and v, but she giggled more than ever, rose, sleeked herself down, and swayed over to Marius, where she nestled kittenishly against him.

'What did he say?' Donald asked.

'I don't know,' I said. 'But I expect it was Catullus. It nearly always is. And rather improper.'

Donald smiled blankly and said it was awful the amount of knowledge one needed, even to get by, and he thought he had better get his overcoat.

All the lesser Peters were stretching themselves and admiring their slim legs and their unobtrusive socks. They were all dressed absolutely right for the occasion, and they knew it, and nothing could detract from their pleasure in themselves. I thought how lucky they were to be young and trim, and the choice, whatever it was, to be theirs; how lucky they were. They were able, too, to join the right clubs. Even not having much money does not stop them; they always have enough for their clubs and their clothes and the achievement of their especial rightnesses. No wonder they held themselves apart; they had no need to come to this kind of party, being in a position, as young men are, particularly such young men, to take their pick of parties. They could even meet anyone they wished to meet without going to any party, ever. In the club, whichever one, there would always be someone who knew someone, who knew the Duchess or the Dowager Duchess, or the Chairman, or the Managing Director, or the man in the back room who really counted, and from then onwards, providing one was young and trim and wore the right socks, one was, so to speak, already made.

They all wore little woolly waistcoats, buff-coloured, as unobtrusive as their socks; thin wool; I believe it used to be called alpaca, and perhaps still is. Only Marius was left in the year before last, wearing a fancy waistcoat, but somehow it was different for him; one felt that he had always worn one, and always would. No doubt all the young men like Donald had taken over the velvet waistcoats, the lush waistcoats, and now the thing was to be drably correct. No, Donald wasn't wearing a waistcoat at all, which, in the circumstances, was very wise. He had enough to do conductoring during the day and learning shorthand and typing at night, without taking on the added burden of what waistcoats were in and what were not. I remembered that Bernhardt did not care either; he had worn a jumper, hand-knitted, which wrinkled around his stomach.

As the Peters made their politely formal, just sufficiently informal, goodbyes, I noticed that they were not exactly 'fonny' in Pisa's way of thought; in fact if any of them had ever been 'fonny' they were growing out of it. They were just not one jot interested. Or if they were, or had tendencies to be, 'fonny', they could stop it – at least on the surface – if it became expedient.

Alexandra still clung with soft tenacity to her one and only Peter.

Having hounded everyone out, and left the way clear for the two of them, I told Alexandra that if she gave me a ring in the morning, I'd come immediately and we'd clear up together.

'You're an angel,' she said. 'I think you've done wonders. But Mrs Aitch, the awful old creature who slops dirty water down the front steps every Saturday, has promised to come in as an "extra". But will you come and have coffee with me about eleven? My red-headed child isn't being brought along until the afternoon – just about fog time – so useful.'

I said I'd try, if I was still alive, and after we had kissed each other, and I had thanked her, and she had thanked me again, and Peter had tried to look debonair and careless, and quite accustomed to being left alone with his hostess long after everyone else had gone, I said that I would let myself out.

'Here, I say, can't I see you home? You can't possibly go off by yourself like that.' Peter really meant it: his upbringing was engrained: he was relieved, though, when I explained that I lived on the ground floor.

I closed the door of the drawing room (which was the dining room and the living room, and the workroom, and all rooms except the bedroom) softly behind me, thinking how clever I was, and hoping that everything would be all right, whichever way Alexandra wanted it. And if I knew her she was a puritan at heart.

There, slumped in the hall chair, fast asleep, was Donald. When I shook him awake he collected himself reasonably quickly, apologized, said that he thought he must have had a drop too much, and allowed himself to be led downstairs. He assured me that he would, quite happily, either find somewhere to sit and wait for the workmen or try to get a lift home, wherever home was.

I did not attempt to persuade him otherwise, not being at my kindest in the early hours of the morning. I could have let him sleep in my hall, but then I might have had to offer him breakfast, which would have been almost intolerable; besides, I had already begun to worry about tomorrow, and to realize – which is always the sharpest blow, the pain of which is not dulled by constant repetition – that tomorrow was now, that very very minute.

My flat was large enough to give a feeling of loneliness; the ceilings were very high, and everywhere was cold and dark. Even when I had switched on all the lights I did not feel much better about it.

I looked at myself in the bathroom mirror, and I could have cried. But after gin and tepid water pinkened by a few drops of bitters, a tumblerful of chilled red wine, and much more brandy than I was accustomed to, I might have felt like crying, anyway. I recalled, sadly, my good resolve to drink grenadine, which, of course, I had left untasted. There are only about five minutes during which I feel sparklingly enlivened by drink, after that despair takes over. I have never succeeded in stopping myself at the crucial moment; either I do not reach it, or, more likely, I go too far.

I washed my face and hands, steeling myself not to give up entirely; decided to do nothing about my hair, threw myself into bed, and prepared myself for a nice long think about Alexandra and Peter. Almost immediately I fell asleep.

2

The Consequences

THE NEXT MORNING I CRAWLED UP TO ALEXANDRA'S flat, without stopping to make myself breakfast first. She said she had not had any either, so we would have coffee and croissants when we had cleared up after Mrs Aitch.

'It was shattering,' said Alexandra, shuddering, 'especially with my head feeling as though lots of wires were broken inside. Mrs Aitch arrived all very noisy and bright at about a quarter to nine, and she's only just gone. She did all the glasses, and got the sticky marks off everywhere, and she's actually polished the furniture. The place smells much better, but she was very hearty and she insisted on telling me what she had for breakfast: fried egg and sausage and lots of fried bread, not drained, but all fatty – that's very important. She says she likes inside work and can't bear doing the steps which is menial, and she thinks we ought to take it in turns to do our own. Except Mr What's-his-name on the floor below. She says there's some things men ought to be put to do, but not steps because that's not their proper place, neither.'

'She must be very popular,' I said.

'Actually she's not a bad old thing,' said Alexandra. 'If only she wasn't so breezy. I'm sure she knew we'd made rather a night of it, and she was hoping for the worst, and no end disappointed because I didn't ask her to make the bed. She was longing to find some signs of licentiousness and probably thought I'd made the bed quick as quick to cover up my traces.'

'And did you?' I asked. 'You can tell me to mind my own business, if you like, but I began to wonder after I'd left you – you do look so very young sometimes, especially when you're tired.'

She smiled. 'Don't worry. I'm no more experienced than I was yesterday, if that's what you mean.'

After that we didn't speak for ten minutes or so while we hunted frantically to find where Mrs Aitch had put things, and to replace them where they ought to be. The room looked as though a heavy gale had blown through it and tossed the lampshades and rugs and pictures and ashtrays and books, and left them all lopsided and not quite as they were before.

Then we settled down to our coffee and croissants and butter, feeling slightly more able to face the day.

'To tell you the truth,' said Alexandra, as she poured out her second cup of coffee, 'I didn't go to bed at all. I just took off my dress and shoes, rolled myself in the eiderdown, and slept on the sofa. I couldn't face a cold bedroom, and I was too exhausted to care, anyway, and the fire was still going strong in here, which was consoling. Peter made it up just before he left.'

She lapsed into a puzzled silence.

'It was all awfully odd, really. He stayed for hours, and we just lay on the sofa – that was before I took my dress off, which I didn't do until he left – and while we were lying there, just being, I felt rather sick, what with the drink, and the excitement, and everything, and I had a simply ghastly headache. Peter was very sweet; he brought me two aspirins and some milk, then he took me in his arms, and I went to sleep. That appalling kind of three-quarters sleep, when you're conscious all the time that your mouth's dry as dust and your eyeballs hurt like mad.'

'And did Peter go to sleep, too?'

'No, I don't think so. I woke up properly once or twice, and I could see his face quite clearly in the firelight. He was just lying there on his back with his eyes wide open.'

'As if he were dead,' I suggested.

'Yes, just as if he were dead. I remember wondering, once, but I could feel his breathing.'

'That must have been a comfort.'

'Not *very*. In fact I might have preferred it if he *had* died. Though I expect I'd have been howling like a vixen by now.'

'Perhaps he was being thoughtful,' I said. 'Quite likely he didn't want to take advantage of you, although he would not put it to himself in such a common way. And quite right, too; you're far too sweet to be taken advantage of, especially after a party, when one is at one's lowest ebb. He sounds a perfectly proper young man, with perfectly proper instincts, and I applaud his restraint and good sense. You'd have felt yourself messily involved this morning, and you'd be wishing it hadn't happened.'

Alexandra threw me a cigarette, and then lit one for herself.

'Doesn't it taste filthy, the first one?' She regarded the cigarette crossly. 'Why do we go on doing it? ... I feel awfully queasy, if that's the word, but more mental than physical. I'm not sure that I wanted Peter actually to do anything – and what with my feeling sick and having a headache fit to burst my head, it would hardly have been a propitious moment – but I must admit that I wanted him to *want* to – if you get my meaning.'

'Perfectly,' I said; 'but perhaps he did want to, and he was only being chivalrous.'

'No-o, I shouldn't have said so; not that I'm so well up in these matters. But he was more forthcoming – you know, hand-pressing, and special smiles, and all the old routine, but it seemed quite new and wonderful because it was Peter – when everyone was here. When we were alone, well, he seemed just a bit frightened.'

'Perhaps he was. He's quite young, too, isn't he? And being well brought up, and perhaps not all that experienced himself, he may not have been sure how far you wanted him to go, and then in the state you were in, the whole thing might have been quite disastrous. And you must remember that anyone who can do anything really well has probably done it lots of times before – but maybe he hasn't and he might have been afraid of making a fool of himself.'

'I haven't either,' she said, and suddenly burst into tears.

It took quite a time before I could soothe Alexandra, because by then she was suffering a double humiliation: first through Peter's cod-like behaviour; second, that she had cried in front of me.

At last all was calm again; I washed up the breakfast things, and Alexandra, who had removed the traces of tears, settled herself with her back to the window, the half-finished pastel portrait on the easel in front of her, doing something with what resembled a stick of tightly rolled newspaper, which she called 'smoothing and softening a bit', preparatory to the child's arrival for the afternoon sitting. Whatever she was doing made the colours look a trifle more blurred, which was not an improvement.

'I'm not really much good at this sort of thing, and yet it's the only sort of thing I can get,' she said. 'And I'm not bad enough for anyone to notice specially, and I'm very very conscientious. I do *try*, heaven knows. But either the little pigs haven't got any expression, or they've got far too much.' She scrubbed away for another few seconds, with the tip of her tongue slightly showing, concentrating intently. Then she said she thought she'd have done better to leave it alone. 'I know someone who knows someone who knows a publisher,' she said, 'who has promised – well, almost – to let me illustrate a tiny little book on cats. I mean it isn't an important book, and I can't do much harm. Do you think I ought to try?'

'Do you like cats?' I asked.

With a tip of tongue still showing, she began to scrub again at the portrait with the stick of rolled newspaper. She shook her head. 'Not really,' she said. 'They jump about so, and dig their claws in everything. I feel they are anti-humans, and ought to be placated, and I never know how to go about it.'

'If I were you I wouldn't take it on, then.'

'It isn't only a question of that. If my work's all right this publisher can put lots of little commissions my way. A friend of mine, though, said he commissioned her to illustrate a book on horses, but he wanted much more than that long before the end. She says he propositioned her practically as soon as she was inside the door, and somehow it doesn't seem fair when work is involved, does it?'

'What did she do? Did she say No, all brisk and virtuous?'

'Well, not exactly. She tried to be awfully cagey and say No, but make it sound as though she meant Maybe, at some other time, when the atmosphere was better. But it entailed a frightful lot of fending off, which wears one out, and she said she thinks he knew he was being fended off and he wasn't taken in. In fact he seemed to take a poorer view than if she'd said No straight away. I suppose all the hanging about had made him peevish. Anyway, he got to be very difficult to deal with; always telling her he didn't like the face of this horse or that one, and would she come and just touch it up, or alter a nostril, or whatever one does to the faces of horses. And then he'd sit and breathe over her, and his breath was always that decaying smell of chlorophyll – although he might have smelled of decay anyway, he's about eighty. And after all that he was mean as mean, and gave her even less than he'd promised – after what she'd had to put up with, too – and then to cut down her royalty was just about the end.'

'Didn't she have a proper contract?'

'Only a kind of letter. One of those beastly friendly arrangements, where you've got to be so much more friendly than you bargained for, otherwise you're out, and you may be out anyway, even if you let them get almost unbearably friendly, because there are always several wives, and what is called Other Interested Parties, somewhere around, and one is sure to get the worst of it.'

'If I were you I'd keep well away from that cat book,' I said. 'It sounds much more trouble than it's worth.'

'That's what I think, really. But one doesn't want to get a reputation for being stuffy, does one?'

'Quite honestly,' I said, 'I don't know. Although somehow I can't imagine that a reputation for not being stuffy, as you put it, would be of much advantage.'

'You sound like an aunt of mine,' said Alexandra, 'who is always telling me to remember not to let myself down. I expect she means not to let her down. But then she lives in Tunbridge Wells.' Alexandra added this as though it ought to make everything miraculously clear.

Soon after that I left her, as she seemed more at ease, and not likely to begin weeping again, and the ceramics and the knitting patterns were weighing heavily on my mind.

After about an hour's exhausted typing on the ceramics, my whole being was irradiated by one glowing idea: I realized that I did not have to understand the wretched thing – I had merely to type it. After that all swam along quite easily.

When I had sent off the ceramics and the knitting patterns I began on a novel, the manuscript of which I had tried to brace myself to look at for several weeks past. It was very long, very intimate in flavour, and the preamble was what the author called his '*dédicace*'; apparently he had come under the influence of Montherlant, Gide, Cocteau, and someone else whose name I could not read. An inauspicious beginning indeed. The palms of my hands began to sweat slightly, and I thought, 'This is it; this is what I have always dreaded; that having undertaken to type a manuscript which, at first glance, was apparently legible, and having put off the work for weeks and weeks, reaching a point when it must be typed without further delay, I shall find that I just cannot read it at all.'

However, when the first panic had subsided I decided that although it was not easy, it was not impossible.

Alexandra did not even visit me for our customary glass of sherry together, and when, about three evenings later, she did present herself, I had no sherry to offer her.

'Never mind, darling,' she said, 'I've brought one of your own bottles of wine – we didn't drink it all the other evening – because I've heard you tapping away madly when I've passed your window, and I thought things might be a bit desperate.'

'Yes,' I said, 'they are. The ceramics man has gone off on some Hellenic cruise, and his secretary says she may be able to obtain special dispensation, or whatever it is called, to draw a cheque on his behalf before he gets back, if it's absolutely urgent – and of course one doesn't want to admit that it *is* pretty urgent. Besides she sounds so snooty. Her voice reminds me of those receptionists in terribly expensive hairdressers, who smile and smile and book appointments, but who wouldn't know what a typewriter looks like. Not that I'm against that. Often I wish that I didn't know what a typewriter looked like, either. The knitting patterns have paid up on the nail, but that didn't go far. I've just embarked on someone's novel now, and I've got a nasty feeling that when it's finished I shall get paid by instalments. It is all about a young man who is very, very poor, and it sounds too true to be much of a comfort.'

'Oh yes, I know exactly how you feel. It's a ghastly sweat to have to worry about money all the time. The red-haired child's mother paid up, but without one word of praise or blame. She just took the thing and stalked off. When that happens it's rather disconcerting. I wished it could have been better, but the child got restive, and her eyes went wrong. In fact she seemed to develop a positive squint towards the end – I expect she was bored, and no wonder – and I had to keep on doing dots and dashes to the eyes to try to get the squint out. Once it gets in one's practically had it. The child became quite chatty about the third sitting, too. But that was when Mamma left her and went off shopping. The last two sittings, though, Mamma just sat and flipped through *Vogue*, and gave great stomach sighs, and kept on glancing at her wristwatch. I suppose she had shopped rather too enthusiastically and couldn't trust herself out any longer. Or perhaps she thought it was high time I put my heart and soul into the damn thing and finished it. Maybe she was afraid that the longer I took the more I'd charge.'

'Isn't it a pity, nowadays, the way people have no faith?'

'Don't talk to me about faith or non-faith. That's a sore point with me. All the children of talking age have listened to Mrs Knight and they go in for deep theological arguments. And just when I was mugging up spaceships and rockets and buying all the Science Penguins and trying to make head or tail of them. One simply can't keep pace.'

'I think you'd find a lot of useful rhetoric comes in Bernard Shaw. If I were you I'd read all the Prefaces and dig out a few salient pros and cons, and you'll be able to deal with practically any infant. I doubt whether the wheel has come round to Shaw yet, so they probably won't have read a word. You'll be able to confuse them and keep them entranced.'

Alexandra seemed to think that this was worth trying.

'I've seen Pisa passing once or twice,' she said. 'Always surrounded by a covey of young men. How she does get her hands on them, doesn't she? You know, the eternal young: brown suits, and biscuit duffles fastened by bits of wood. Very tasteful.'

'Easy to cope with, I expect. Any interest to you?'

Alexandra blew her nose thoughtfully, and polished the tip.

'I only really like the kind of middling young men who wear bowler hats,' she said at last.

'I suppose if you got hold of a young man who didn't,

you could always see that he bought himself the right kind of bowler. Couldn't you?'

Alexandra shook her head. 'No, that wouldn't do at all. He must be the sort of young man who works things out for himself, and who does wear a bowler, quite quite naturally.'

'Yes, I know. Someone who's been born to it.'

She nodded, and we had another glass of Bordeaux each. It was a wine which took one by the throat for the first glass, then suddenly one gave in, and after the second glass there was just the slightest coldness down the spine, and the real deep shudder did not come again.

Alexandra looked thinner, but very sweet and young in a dark-blue woollen dress, fastening sideways with large pearl buttons from the high neckline to the hem; her light-brown hair was smoothed back; her fingernails were oval-tipped and unvarnished.

Quite obviously there was something she wanted to say, and she had not yet managed to get around to it. She polished the tip of her small nose again, and accepted a cigarette.

'I wonder what people did with their hands before they smoked?' she said. 'It must have been very nerve-racking.'

'I expect they made graceful gestures taking bonbons out of little boxes.'

'Yes, but having taken them out, one would feel under an obligation to eat them. And then to lace one's corsets even tighter. It must have been just as bad as smoking, only in a different way.'

'I expect,' I said, 'there was always something bad going on, but we bring it out in casual conversation, and they didn't. They had to keep it for their memoirs, which shows a good backbone of restraint, although it couldn't have been much fun.'

'Talking about bowler hats,' said Alexandra, although we had not been talking about them for some few minutes, 'I shall be away this weekend.'

I thought furiously. 'Peter?' I asked. '*The* Peter?'

'Yes, *the* Peter.'

'And will he be wearing the traditional bowler as though he were born and bred to it?'

Her face glimmered with amusement. 'I hope not. Not in the kind of car he's got. He's a photographer – did you know? – I mean professionally, for lots of newspapers, or maybe magazines, I'm not awfully well up in the details – and he's got an assignment, or whatever it is called – to photograph some sort of procession which happens only once every fifty years, or it may be once every hundred years, I forget. Anyway, it's something quite special, and he can do it in the rich grand way. The awful thing is I've forgotten exactly what it is: either it's at Glastonbury, something to do with the Thorn, or Shakespeare at Stratford, or it's all Dickensian at Tewkesbury, or somewhere like that. Actually I was so stunned that I could only hear what concerned me, and I couldn't take in the rest. Anyway, he's asked me to go with him, and although I don't know exactly what it means, I've said Yes. After all, it might turn out to be quite perfect, and even if it doesn't one would never forgive oneself for turning down the chance. I mean, not knowing is the worst, isn't it?'

Somewhat dubiously I agreed. I began to wish that Alexandra had a closer relative – closer both by blood ties and by distance – than an aunt who lived in Tunbridge Wells. I felt, that an aunt who lived in Tunbridge Wells might have forgotten what it was like to be young and very unsure of oneself. I had almost forgotten, too, what it was like, having aged immeasurably owing to the ceramics, and the gas account (still unpaid), and the electricity account due any day, and the telephone account which would probably arrive later in the week.

'I've got a nice woolly car rug, left over from the time when I used to have a car,' I said. 'Perhaps you'd like to take that?'

Alexandra accepted, and there we left the subject.

On Saturday morning Alexandra came in to tell me that she was just going off. She looked very gay and not a bit as though she were going to a fate worse than death. She wore a tiny blue velvet hat, a coat of soft tweed, blue-speckled, smelling pleasantly tweedlike, and rather unsuitably high-heeled shoes, to make her look taller.

'I can't walk far in them,' she confided, 'without falling flat on my face. But I'm not going in for long country rambles – at least I hope not. So perhaps it won't matter.'

'Don't you think you ought to take another pair, just in case?' I suggested.

'I've got a rather fetching pair of velvet slippers with little sparklers all over the toes, which can be bedroom slippers, or not, so at least I can put those on in the hotel.'

'What else are you taking?' I asked.

She opened her weekend case and showed me a blue nylon dress which had a pleated skirt, a pair of red-flannel pyjamas, gay, but not exactly provocative, and a large Jaeger shawl in case the nylon frock became intolerably draughty. There were also two volumes of *Splendeurs et Misères des Courtisanes* and a lumping French dictionary.

'You seem to have thought of nearly everything,' I said. Then at my suggestion she took out the second volume of Balzac – it seemed hardly likely that she would read both, even if she read practically continuously the whole time – and she accepted the loan of a small fur cape instead of the shawl. We both agreed that it would look better and take up less room.

By this time Peter was hooting impatiently outside, and I scurried after her to wave them farewell. It was a low-slung car, cream-coloured, with red upholstery. It looked very smart and rather fun, and I could see that the car added to Peter's status, and he became the kind of person with whom one might go away for the weekend, and damn the consequences.

They drove off quite early, and when they had gone I felt rather sorry for myself.

As I turned back to the house, there was Mrs Aitch, doing her weekly slop-and-mop over the front steps. I longed for company, any company, even Mrs Aitch's, and I thought of what a mess my flat was in, and I felt lethargically disinclined to try to clear it up myself, and I remembered that even Keats had had to get everything neat and tidy, and himself spruced up, before he could work. I decided that that might apply equally to typing someone else's manuscripts. After all, it is all work, whether one is doing it first hand or redoing it for other people. So I asked Mrs Aitch whether, as a special favour, she could spare me an hour or two after she'd done the steps.

'All right, dear. But I've got to be off at twelve sharp, see? If my old man doesn't get 'is bit of fish at one, and that means one, he'll create. And I'm off to my daughter's – the married one – this afternoon, so I've got to keep 'im sweet.'

I said that would do fine, and as I went back into the flat I wondered whether I could smell drains, unless it was that decaying clump of shrubs in what was supposed to be the garden. And I remembered that once, and not so long ago, I had lived in the country, and how clean and grassy the air smelled, and I could have howled, grief-stricken, except that it is awful to cry alone, and I did not fancy being comforted by Mrs Aitch. So I went in and made my bed and put out the teacups, ready for a nice cosy chat with Mrs Aitch, who would be better than no one.

'Gives you the bloody 'ump, don't it, these basements?' Mrs Aitch asked cheerfully. 'O' course these 'ouses weren't built for this kind o' thing, and it stands to reason they aren't convenient, see? There's Miss What's-'er-name, your friend, living in them bloody attics wot ought to be maids' quarters, and you livin' in wot ought to be pantries and kitchens.' She drank her tea with enjoyment, and we both had some more.

'Yes, ta,' she said. 'I'd like a fag. My old man don't believe in it, but I say I work fer wot I get and I can bloody well do as I like with my own money, and I mean to, I can tell you.' She sniffed, twitching her nose. 'S'damp in 'ere, ain't it? Thought so. Always damp in them basements, and you can't do nothing about it . . . You live alone?'

I nodded.

'An' I can't say you mightn't be better off, unless you turn the thumbscrew on pronto.'

I said I thought I was fairly set in my ways, and would not need to worry about such things.

Mrs Aitch appraised me competently; took in my hair, combed hours previously, and not since; my shoes, unpolished. 'You be careful, though. My sister-in-law's just married for the first time, and *she's* fifty-seven. You never know when it's going to 'it you.'

I said no, you didn't, and we went our ways – Mrs Aitch to scrub the kitchen floor, which she did merrily, and with a will, and me to tidy my bedroom, which always mysteriously untidies itself five minutes later.

'If I was you,' Mrs Aitch called out friendlily, triumphing

over the rhythmic swish of the scrubbing-brush, 'I'd 'ave all that 'air off. Not that you 'aven't got it done nice, and all that, but I always say it makes you look twice your age with all that 'air plaited about. It stands ter reason, don't it, your 'ead must be so 'eavy – must quite wear you out.'

'I'll think about it,' I said, placatingly.

'Think about it!' Mrs Aitch was contemptuous. 'That's all some people do nowadays, think, think, think. As I said to my daughter the other day – the married one – when she was talking about moving to one o' them new towns, "Go on and do it, that's if you want to, or you won't get no other chance. You'll think yourself into your grave, that you will, my girl." If you do a thing it's no end bucking up.'

Mrs Aitch finished the kitchen floor and began on the inside of the windows.

'All this smog, or whatever they calls it,' she said, 'don't 'alf make a mess, and it's more cheerful like if you can see out, no matter what you're looking at. There's too many windows in a place o' this sort, specially fer nowadays. Needs an army ter look after the 'ouse proper. Not that taken all in all you 'aven't kep' this flat better'n most, and you livin' alone when mostly they don't bother. Some o' them places round 'ere, filthy isn't in it, you wouldn't believe. And nice people, too, real nice people, and 'ow they can live in that muck beats me. Fer instance there's Mrs B in wot used ter be the Grange, round the corner, all togged up, and out to play the flim-flams every afternoon –'

'Mrs Aitch,' I interrupted firmly, 'I'm going out shopping now, but I won't be long.'

'S'all right,' she said, helping herself to another of my cigarettes. I can't say I grudged her.

I met Pisa coming down the hill as I was going up. She

looked existentialist in the neatest cleanest way. She wore some kind of trews, slick to the thighs and narrowing to the ankle, and a little short jacket, bright green, and very Bavarian. Her hair was taken right back and looped and braided at the nape of her neck; she wore no make-up except lipstick, and she looked like a good child. Disconcertingly beautiful, and younger than anything one could possibly imagine. She gave me a wide shining smile.

'Now we have coffee and cake? Pisa knows just the place, very near. You come, please?'

Her smile, her affectionate, if meaningless, friendliness, were irresistible. I said Yes, but I couldn't stay long because I had to get back to pay Mrs Aitch.

Pisa led me swiftly to a small dark cafe, run by a small dark man. The cakes were very rich, consisting, as far as I could make out, of mounds of banana-flavoured cream sitting on small triangles of flaky pastry. It was difficult to know how one could eat them with the least disaster.

'Good?' Pisa asked.

I nodded. 'Very good.'

'I see your friend who give lovely party,' she said, then paused to wipe off some of the cream around her mouth, 'driving off in chic car with that nice young man, Peter. She is in love with him?'

I said I didn't know.

'Fonny thing about England,' said Pisa, 'people don't know. We always know. Perhaps not for ever, but we know. Plenty of excitement, lots of fun.'

I said maybe it was the different climate. We couldn't be absolutely sure.

She laughed; a high sweet controlled laughter, which she must have taken trouble to acquire – and very effective it was.

'Very serious in England.' She pulled down her mouth. 'You watch; you wait; and nothing happen. We laugh. Everything happen very very quickly. Then we cry a lot, and everything happen over again but with someone different. Good fun.'

'Yes, if you've got the stamina,' I said. Obviously she had.

She patted her stomach. 'Pisa tough as old boot, so someone said.'

I wondered who.

'Pisa very very unhappy.' She became pathetic. 'Working for old sow. Even her husband do not deny she is old sow,' she added disinterestedly.

'What a jolly household,' I said.

'Poo,' she said, jolly as hell, that I tell you. 'I come here to learn English. She knows that. But she says Cook this, and cook that, and mend this and mend that, and then make curtains. So I say Poo, and she say, "Get out, you rude young woman," so I say, "You go to hell, you old sow." Her husband laugh, and she have kind of fit.' Pisa helped herself to another cake and held out my cup, then her own, for more coffee, gave the impervious young man behind the counter a ravishing smile, before she continued. 'So she is taken off, and husband say, "You quite right, Pisa, but you must go before she return."' Pisa sighed and added dispiritedly, 'And she return next week.'

'Then I suppose you'll have to get out?' I asked, off my guard.

Her mouth drooped. 'Nowhere to go. Nowhere. I am very clever, very clean. You have big flat?'

'Not very.' A dreadful clamminess came over me. 'And I haven't any money. Really, not *any* money.'

'Is no matter.' She was forgiving. 'Pisa just want somewhere to sleep, until Pisa get job again. I don't like women – but you're different. Simpatica.'

'That's too easy,' I said.

'Please?' Pisa put on her lost-child expression.

'No, Pisa, I'm sorry but –' I began.

'Don't say,' Pisa begged. 'Pisa pay here, and then we walk and walk and talk, and get friends. No?'

I had forgotten Pisa's yearning for long long walks. I thought of Mrs Aitch's husband who'd create if he didn't get his fish at one sharp, and the young man's novel waiting to be typed, and how I had meant to wash my hair. Pisa took my arm and set off with feline easy strides towards the Heath. Oh, heavens, I thought, she really *is* one for the great open spaces. She managed to look different, too; a fascinating entrapping blend of a female Borrow and a George Sand. This was obviously her Heath personality, turned on full force for my benefit. I took it as a compliment – as she had intended – knowing that seldom did she set out to ensnare a woman. Even if she has nowhere to sleep, I told myself weakly, there must be *something* about me ... By then the battle was nearly over.

I don't, to this day, know exactly how it happened; twice round the pond, with Pisa, tall and lithesome, purposefully grasping my arm, and talking intently, and towards the end of the second circuit I had already agreed to let Pisa come and stay with me until she found somewhere to go.

'But mind,' I added quaveringly, trying to take a stand when it was too late, 'it can't be for long, Pisa, because I might want to ask someone else to come and stay, and there's only one spare room.'

Pisa winked, and then I remembered Pisa's wink at the party, and I felt that I ought to have been forewarned.

'Pisa understand. Pisa sleep anywhere. Pisa so so grateful she lie doggo – that right word? – on *mat* if essential.'

I assured her that that would not be essential, and we parted with mutual expressions of goodwill. Pisa said she would 'bring herself in' tomorrow night, and she would dust and shop and cook, and even make curtains for me, if I wanted her to.

I walked home and I wished that Alexandra were there, and I could at least have told her all about it, and we would have laughed together. As it was, I would have to face a cross Mrs Aitch.

Although it was well past twelve, Mrs Aitch wasn't cross, and had apparently forgotten all about her old man and his bit of fish, which was a blessing. She cut short my apologies.

'Never you mind, dear,' she said. 'I've just finished the cupboard under the sink, and it didn't 'alf niff, I can tell you. When you throw things in the bin, throw them careful, see?'

I promised that I would throw them careful, and I gave her a shilling extra and two cigarettes, and she said she would pop in next Saturday to make sure I didn't want nothing. I thought that if the worst came to the worst, Mrs Aitch could always be prevailed upon to put Pisa out, bag and baggage, and be glad, no doubt, to do it.

I made myself some sandwiches, drank a glass of the wine which Alexandra had left behind, shuddered violently, tried to type, gave it up. The combination of Mrs Aitch and Pisa in one morning had curdled inside me.

I thought about Alexandra and Peter, and I wondered what they were doing, and I hoped they were happy. I remembered her silly, pretty, high heels, and I wondered whether her feet ached, and I hoped so very much that she was finding it all worth it; worth the weighing up, and the excitement, and the getting ready, and the strain of going off. I hoped, too, that they would find happiness together in the night time, and that mere nothings would not trip them up; dripping taps, and chilly rooms; indifferent food; surly suspicious chambermaids; and all the attendant minor miseries which people have continually to fight against. And love, especially a new untried one, cannot laugh at these small disasters. Affection, a shared life, a steady settled relationship, these can overcome the lesser evils of discomfort, possibly embarrassment, but love alone cannot do so.

Then I pulled myself together, made some tea, and got down to the novel. My day had been thoroughly disorganized.

About nine o'clock Bernhardt arrived.

'May I come in?' he asked, walking past me and seating himself by the fire. His English was perfect; obviously he was in complete command of himself.

'How did you know where I lived?'

'I have just met Pisa,' he said. 'She told me your address and that she is coming to live with you.'

'She told you *what*? Now listen, she is coming to stay with me, for as short a time as possible, until she finds herself somewhere else to go. And when she gets a job she'll "live in" presumably. I like Pisa but –'

He grinned. 'Don't worry,' he said. 'We will work it out when it gets difficult for you. I must explain that I am studying her. I am studying all women. For my survey. Now my survey is a serious piece of work on which I have been working on for years, and I am damned sick of people smiling and lifting the eyebrows.'

'No doubt,' I said, smiling meanly and lifting the eyebrows further.

'Pisa is an extrovert type of the very first group – I use simple untechnical language so that you may follow – and as such a rarity. It is seldom found that a woman fits one group, and one only. It is more usual that, like you, they are bits of every group and not easy to classify. But you have a special interest for me, being the personification of the perfect example of pure guilt: maybe guilt for what you have done; or what you have not done; or what you do not do; or maybe guilt referred to now for what you will do in the future.'

I said that sounded fairly comprehensive, and I couldn't see any loophole I could wriggle out of.

'Very comprehensive,' he agreed. 'Otherwise, why call it a survey?'

'Why indeed?' I said. 'The one possibility which you seem to have overlooked is that my guilt is concerned with what I am doing now, in the present.'

'Very interesting, very interesting.' He was excited and lost his command of English again. 'Not many women would be so quick on the up-put.' His eyes were bright with the researcher's frenzy. 'But no, I do not think you do what causes you to feel guilt in the present. That possibility I studied with care at your friend's party.'

'Surely you can't judge from a party? I wouldn't be behaving guiltily then, in any case, would I?'

I was tired of the novel which had to be typed; tired of sandwiches and weak tea and cheap wine. Tired of living alone (although Pisa's presence did not appear the ideal solution); tired of the misery of losing interest in myself; tired of the seemingly incessant winter: tired of the old, old Mid-European theories of this wretched man, who really thought that he was doing me a favour by discussing me in large and general terms, who really expected me to get excited about his survey. And yet, I thought, it was pleasant to have someone there, even Bernhardt was better than spending the rest of the evening by myself.

'You do not understand.' He beamed with pleasure. There is nothing which so gratifies a man who has some peculiar theory of his own to expound, as a woman not understanding. It is exactly what he has waited for and what he can immediately grasp. 'I do not speak of guilt in particular terms of what you do, or say, or think, or desire, at such an hour, on such a day. I speak of guilt as the general impact which you force upon the serious student of women: guilt as one of your foremost qualities. It is very interesting, and not much met with.'

I said I was glad to hear that there was something about me not much met with.

'You laugh?' He was reproachful. 'Englishwomen always refuse to discuss primary causes. It is their first defence against men.'

'Pisa says just the opposite. She told me that Englishwomen don't take things lightly enough – especially men.'

'So,' he said. 'That is most instructive. Two types, you and Pisa, entirely opposed. Most instructive.'

He was silent for a few minutes, then came to a grudging conclusion: 'You have eaten?'

'Not really.'

'I know nice quiet warm little café just around the corner. We go there and we talk, and then we come back, and we talk some more. Yes?'

'Which little café?' I asked suspiciously.

He told me. 'Lovely cakes, real coffee as made in Vienna.'

'I know, I know,' I said. 'Banana-flavoured cream and very thick cups. I've had some. Pisa took me there this morning.'

'You not like it?'

'No,' I said firmly. 'I not like it. If you want to survey me, you've got to play it my way. Besides, it's too cold, and I don't want to go out, and in any case I'm too old for cream cakes at this time of night. The very idea turns me up, and that's a new expression for you.'

'What shall we do? You want to cook? We eat here?' He was trying hard to work it out.

'No, certainly not. You go to the delicatessen just across the road, and you buy some smoked salmon sandwiches – the *best* smoked salmon, mind, because they've got imitation something all ready cut up and sealed in little bags which isn't salmon at all. Then when they've made the sandwiches you ask them to cut the crusts off. After that you go into the Jug and Bottle at the Three Feathers, and you buy a half-bottle of Pouilly at six shillings and ninepence, or if you feel lavish a whole bottle of Pouilly at eleven shillings and sixpence. Then you come back, and we can eat and drink, and you may ask me whatever questions – within reason – you wish.' While I had been talking Bernhardt had obediently made one or two notes, anxious not to forget his programme.

'So,' he said thoughtfully. 'What is Jog and Bottle?'

'Never mind,' I said, 'you just go to the door which has Jug and Bottle written on it. That's where you buy the wine.'

'All right.' Suddenly he entered into the spirit of the thing. He felt that he was taking part in an adventure.

'Bye-bye.' He waved from the doorway, as though I were a child, and he was trying to make me watch the dicky bird.

'Bye-bye,' I found myself saying, fatuously, flapping my hand at him.

He returned quite soon, having executed the commissions most faithfully. It was the best smoked salmon; the crusts were cut off; and he had managed to buy the right Pouilly – a bottle.

I praised him extravagantly, and he was apparently very

pleased. As we sat and ate the sandwiches and drank the wine he became quite human, and did not once mention his survey. He told me about Vienna, and how much he had loved the city, and exactly why he did not want to return there, ever (there were many reasons all of which I have completely forgotten), and how he suffered from rheumatism at that time of the year, and how well his landlady looked after him, even buying his underwear.

I told him about the novel I was typing, and he said, 'Montherlant, pah! With these young ones it is always Montherlant. He does much harm that man with his *malignes faussetés*. One big toad, yes, but all the little toadpoles, no.'

When he left he bowed and kissed my hand, and we both said, many times, how much we had enjoyed the evening – which, for my part at least, was true.

I began to feel that even Pisa's arrival the next day might not turn out as badly as I had expected.

Pisa brought herself in, as she said she would. She had a large fibre suitcase and an enormous basketwork holdall with wooden handles. Just the kind of large unwieldy basket which one always wants to buy abroad, but on the last day cannot, perhaps fortunately, afford.

She was very quiet and subdued.

'It is very kind,' she said, almost pathetically. 'Very good of you to take Pisa in. I go unpack, and sit in my room. No, I do not take anything, thank you.'

Then with a little half-bow she presented me with a sweet tightly folded bunch of lilies of the valley which she had taken out from the top of the basket. When I thanked her we stared, transfixed, at each other; a terrible welling sympathy threatened to swamp us both, but we had enough good sense to control it. Pisa scurried into her own room, and I fled back to my typewriter, shutting the door firmly behind me.

I bet that woman really *is* an old sow, I thought, and began to type furiously.

The next morning I found that Pisa had laid my breakfast tray, with all the wrong china on it, but it looked very nice, all neat and ready for me. There, in the middle of the tray, was a tiny blue glass in which was a spray of carefully washed laurel leaves – pilfered no doubt from some nearby hedge – and leaning against the glass was a note in painstakingly upright script: *To Mifs Marianne: Am taking Mfs. Vassenheimer's animale for vork beck later – gracias thenks Pisa.*

Evidently Pisa had a life of which I knew nothing I wondered what Mrs Vassenheimer's animale was, and rather hoped that I would not have the chance of finding out – at least not just yet. Any animale is likely to cause added chaos in an already disjointed household.

Soon after I had finished breakfast Pisa returned, gleaming and beaming after her encounter with Mrs Vassenheimer's animale and their romp together in the cold, frost-crisp air.

The animale was a poodle, – 'big as this', she said, showing me how big with her hands. According to Pisa it was about the size of a pony. Pisa and the poodle had met a water rat by the edge of the pond, which had made their morning. She seemed to find the water rat most attractive.

'Sixty and five, perhaps, vater-rats like that one – big and fat,' she said, 'would make lovely short jacket. Simple to skin and bake in oven. I would prepare myself.'

'Oh no, Pisa! Certainly not. That I simply won't have. You must not bring one water rat, mind you, not one, near this place. If you do, then it is the end between us.'

'As you please.' She was obviously disappointed. 'But it was to be my present. I say to that damn silly dog, "You catch vater rat", and damn dog run away.'

'Mrs Vassenheimer,' I said firmly, 'wouldn't want her poodle to have anything to do with a water rat. That I'm sure of.'

'Perhaps not.' Pisa shrugged her shoulders. 'But she would not know. She is dead out until two o'clock or maybe three. She just sleep and sleep. She give it to herself, you know.' Pisa picked up a fork and pretended to stab herself in the thigh.

'Do you mean she gives herself injections?' I asked, feeling somewhat bewildered. Mrs Vassenheimer, even at second hand, was going to be an added complication.

'But yes.' Pisa sounded astounded at my slowness. 'I thought everyone do it after certain age, and she is much after certain age. Most women after forty have substitute for sex cycle.'

'Don't be silly, Pisa,' I said. 'You know perfectly well that is just nonsense.'

Suddenly she smiled widely. 'Yes,' she said, 'damn nonsense. Mrs Vassenheimer's doctor pricked me, too, but I just felt fonny and very, very tired, and everything went very long when I looked at it. That was all that happen.' Indifferently, as though it were a matter of no moment, Pisa rolled up the sleeve of her sweater, and there on her forearm were little spots as though pins had been stuck in just far enough to draw blood.

I looked, and then I looked again; yes, there was no mistake.

'Pisa,' I said sternly. 'As long as you stay here you will give me your word that you will not go near Mrs Vassenheimer's doctor. And I hope you won't, even if you don't stay here. And no water-rats, either.'

'Please?' Pisa put on her most innocent and unknowing expression, and then, finding me unmoved, said reluctantly: 'I give both my words if you wish.'

Obviously trying to make amends, she insisted on washing up the breakfast things.

I gave Pisa the spare key to the front door, and then took myself back to the young man's novel which, hour by hour, was becoming more of a burden to me.

I heard Alexandra return; her thin high-heeled shoes tapped lightly and quickly up the stairs as the car which had apparently brought her back was restarted again with a hurtful crash of a clumsy gear change.

That evening, just after six, Alexandra arrived, carrying a bottle of sherry, Tio Pepe, a tin of Bath Oliver biscuits, and a small jar of Stilton.

'Will this do?' she asked. She was more carefully made up than usual, her eyes shone, the pupils seemed overlarge, as though with belladonna; her lipstick, too, was brighter.

'Do? Why, it's absolute heaven. May we just sit and eat and drink?'

She nodded, well pleased with the success of her presents.

The Stilton and Tio Pepe tasted so good that for a few minutes we concentrated upon them and did not speak.

'You tell me first,' she said. 'Everything smells different here, as though lots had been happening.'

So I curbed my impatient curiosity, and told her all about Mrs Aitch, and how Bernhardt had arrived unexpectedly, and the smoked salmon sandwiches, and then about Pisa, and Mrs Vassenheimer's animale, and Mrs Vassenheimer's doctor, and the pricks on Pisa's arm, and how, although it was quite absurd and to some extent inconvenient, I did not even want to try to turn Pisa out, because she was Pisa and fundamentally rather different from what she appeared, and because of the lilies of the valley, and the laurel leaves, and because she seemed so young, and walked at such a pace, and because she insisted on buying me Viennese coffee and beastly cream cakes.

Alexandra understood perfectly. 'It is a bore,' she agreed, 'but you'll just have to keep her until you settle her somewhere else, or until she settles herself.'

'Yes,' I said. 'Isn't it appalling? And yet it's good in a way; an indication that one is still part, however remotely, of a positive life. So often everything seems negative, and the whole of one's time consists of what hasn't been done. I get to the state when I actually recall the days or months, or even years, the whole divisions of life, by what hasn't been done. I find myself thinking: yes, that was the summer I didn't get to Italy; or that was the Christmas I didn't send any cards. Then there are always the books I mean to read, and the friends I mean to get in touch with – all adding up to a monstrous chase where the hare's always a different one, but always gets away.'

'Oh, darling, I know, I know,' she said. 'It's all a question of discipline, I expect. Or it may be a question of something which we don't take any account of nowadays, or at least I don't. Perhaps there is something in belief, and if we had it everything would be better. But one can't just suddenly decide to go to church because one wants to ask for a lot of things, can one? It would seem so weak and unmannerly, wouldn't it?'

We had some more sherry and some more Stilton, and several more cigarettes, and we enjoyed the blessed quiet of the house. If Pisa was in, we could not hear her. Which was a relief. She was pleasant to consider in retrospect, but I did not want her to become all-pervading.

I noticed that Alexandra was smoking quickly and nervously.

'And you?' I asked at last, judging that a sufficiently decent interval had elapsed. 'Has all gone well with you?'

'It depends what you mean by going well,' she said, sounding rather perplexed. 'I don't yet know where Peter was bound for, or whether he was bound for anywhere. We drove for miles and miles. Saturday was heaven; everything bright and shining, and the roads glittered, and the sky was pale pink, and Peter held my hand, while he drove with his other, and we talked and laughed a lot. Something went wrong just about lunchtime because we didn't find the right kind of place before we were hungry, and then when we were hungry there wasn't the right kind of place, not anywhere. And we went on and on, and in the end we bought cheese and bread and two little pork pies and a large bunch of grapes and a bottle of wine, and even then we couldn't seem to agree on where we should stop to eat it, which was quite absurd, because there were so many places, all quiet and glowing and wintry, but in the nicest way.'

'However nice it may have looked, it sounds far too cold for a picnic, to me,' I said.

'I'm always a bit frightened of hashed-up things, too, and I had a wild idea that the pork pies were stale, and I still think they were. And Peter got mad and threw them down on the road and backed the car over them. I suppose that was just temper, but I didn't feel like applauding. Then after the wine, and not eating much, I began to wonder what I was doing, anyway, in a small car with Peter in the middle of the Cotswolds, with a suitcase, and not knowing where we were going. It all became terribly unreal, and in spite of the heater and rugs I was chilled through.'

'And did you arrive anywhere?' I asked.

She smiled. 'In the sense of place, of course we did. I think I must have dozed and I was stiff with cold and tiredness, and it was heaven when we got there, because there were enormous fires and hot buttered toast for tea.'

I didn't ask where, thinking it better, perhaps, not to know.

'The inn was very old and tucked away; not even in a village; and Peter seemed more at ease, perhaps because he had found a nice little house for his car, and he'd covered the radiator over with an old sack which he keeps in the boot, and patted the bonnet, and fussed around it, as though it were a person he was bedding down for the night. That was when I realized we were to stay there, although I suppose it did depend to some extent on me, as I think he asked me after tea whether I'd be happy to stay or if I wanted to "push on". I felt I never wanted to move again, what with the fire, and the buttered toast, and an enormous sleepiness coming over me. But I longed to wash and put myself to rights, as it were, and to find out exactly where I was – at least metaphorically.'

At that moment there was the noise of Pisa's arrival, and another voice which I seemed to know.

'I'd better go and see what's happening,' I said. 'Pisa's rather an unknown quantity at the moment.'

Alexandra nodded. 'And try and fend them off, there's a darling,' she suggested anxiously. 'It's much cosier, just the two of us, and I don't feel I want to cope.'

I said neither did I.

I found Pisa hovering in the passage. She pounced upon me.

'I met Marius and bring him back. He is in my room. All right? You permit?'

I said certainly I permitted, if he were in her room for unexceptionable purposes.

She looked reproachfully at me. 'We have coffee and we make music,' she said. 'That is all right?'

I said it would be perfectly all right, but not too much music, and not too loud, otherwise Mr What's-his-name on the first floor would make a fuss, and I'd get it in the neck from the landlord.

'Lots of coffee and little music,' she agreed meekly.

'I don't much mind Marius, but I do draw the line at Mummy,' I said, as an afterthought, just in case Pisa might decide at some future encounter to ask Mummy back too.

Pisa gave a tinkling laugh. 'Mummy jdamn bore,' she said feelingly. 'But Marius must not know.'

I said I thought he did know, and he was trying to make the best of it.

Pisa considered this, then gave a wide delighted smile, as though this had not occurred to her.

'You think I could get Marius away from Mummy?' she asked.

'Only over Mummy's dead body,' I said. 'But don't let that give you any borgiastic ideas. Marius isn't worth that. And besides, you wouldn't get away with it. You're far too attractive to be believed.'

'Silly Marianne, how fonny you are.' She gave an affectionate clutch at my arm and danced off.

I returned to Alexandra, who was staring moodily at the fire.

'That was Pisa,' I explained. 'She's got Marius in tow, and quite by mistake I seem to have given her the mad idea of tearing him away from Mummy.'

Alexandra cheered up and giggled. 'What a hope,' she said. 'Poor Marius, he'll have to do penance for this tomorrow.

It'll be the confessional for him at six sharp, *and* on an empty stomach. Then he'll get one of his interminable colds, and he'll keep on sniffing drops of this and that up his nose, and he'll have to carry a briefcase of paper handkerchiefs absolutely everywhere. Remorse and confession at the crack of dawn always bring on one of his colds.'

She was silent for a few minutes. 'I don't want to lose Marius for ever and ever,' she said. 'It's nice to have someone on tap, as it were, to take one out occasionally, and he does do things properly – when he does them, which isn't, alas, often; what with his nearly always being a bit under the weather, and what with Mummy. But when he does them it's always the third row of the stalls, right in the centre, and the right kind of supper afterwards – I mean the oysters and champagne kind, if I wanted them, although I don't happen to like either. But it is the real thing; with dressing up and smiling commissionaires, and waiters tipped well, but not too well. All wonderfully relaxing. So, of course, one wouldn't willingly stand aside and say, "After you", and let Pisa scoop the lot, would one?'

'I don't think you need worry,' I said. 'I'm sure Pisa will behave herself. She knows I wouldn't stand for *that*.'

'If you mean by that what I think you mean, I don't imagine Marius would, either.' Alexandra chuckled. 'I've never tried, but somehow one can't see him enjoying even a romp with real abandon. I think all his animal instincts – if any – have been pretty well subdued by Mummy, and I don't suppose there's much left.'

'Anyway,' I said, 'as long as Pisa stays here it's up to her not to set out on any voyages of discovery, and I think I've made that pretty plain. She assures me they're going to make coffee and music, which sounds harmless enough.'

'Marius must be smitten to some extent, because he never drinks coffee in the evening. He says it keeps him awake.'

I was getting a bit sick of Marius by this time, so I said no more.

'Shall I go on?' Alexandra asked.

'I just didn't want to put you off by being too anxious,' I admitted.

'Try to stop me,' she said. 'I must tell someone, and I'd rather tell you, and besides there isn't anyone else I could tell properly. It was all so peculiar – very exciting and quite unsatisfactory. When people say things happened as though it were a dream I've always thought that so pseudo, and I've never believed it, but that's exactly what it *was* like. Which only shows that one ought to be frightfully tolerant and believe absolutely everyone, doesn't it?'

I said I thought that was going a bit too far, but I saw roughly what she meant.

'It was all such a confusion, and Peter muttered something about having arranged everything, and I was shown up into the most heavenly room – very old and beamy, but not ye olde, all quite genuine, and smelling of home-made furniture polish, which nearly made me weep, being such a special smell of childhood, and country houses, and I didn't know I'd ever remembered it, until I smelled it again, and then I knew that it was one of those things I'd lost for a long time.'

At that moment thin, high sounds filtered through to us. Sad, soft, medieval sounds which were not of this world.

'What in God's name is that?' I asked. Somehow I did not immediately connect the sounds with Pisa's threat of making music.

'Oh, that? Of course you haven't heard it before. That's

Marius and his recorder. It's his snake-charming act, and it works, in a mild way, because one is quite impressed the first time. It's the unexpectedness, no doubt. Other people may have lots of things, but only Marius has a recorder – at least other people *may* have recorders, but one doesn't come across them. After the first time it definitely begins to pall, because Marius goes on making the same noises, and they're always so frightfully wistful that one can hardly bear it. Besides he looks so odd and intent when he's playing the thing, and his eyes pop a bit, and it's obviously a ghastly strain.'

We listened for a few minutes. The piping noises suddenly ceased, then Marius began again, apparently on the same dirge.

'I don't know if he's supposed to be playing one particular piece,' I said, 'or whether he makes it up as he goes along. But it certainly lacks something, doesn't it?'

'Practically everything. It might be better if Marius had a little bit of an ear for music, but if he had he probably wouldn't play the beastly thing at all. It even gives Mummy the droops – he told me so. I think it's his only defence against her, although he doesn't know that he needs one.'

'Do let's try to forget Marius – and Mummy,' I said. 'I'm longing to hear about you and Peter.'

'Well, I'll tell you *all* – actually much less than I expected. Somehow the whole weekend was a surprise to both of us. I was just telling you about my room, wasn't I? Lovely old furniture, and the right kind of chintzy curtains, and a real live fire flaring away in an enormous stone hearth; the sort of fireplace in which you can burn two or three trees, practically whole, and you just leave the ash to accumulate, then you put on another tree the next morning, give it a couple of puffs with the bellows, and could soon roast an ox – or at least a sucking pig. It was the genuine thing in every way. Proper old-world comfort.'

'And was there proper old-world discomfort, too?'

'How right you are! No water laid on; it all had to be brought from the one and only bathroom, which was about half a mile away, up and down little steps and along rickety passages, in large brass water jugs which were delivered and left coyly outside the door. I nearly broke myself in half lifting them and pouring them into the ewer, or whatever it is called. But the fire made up for everything, and I had a quite satisfactory standing-up bath, toasting myself at the same time, and then put everything on again, just as I was, because the inn didn't seem to match nylon dresses – much more like tweeds and brogues and shooting-sticks. Anyway, I felt much better when I made up my face again, and soaked myself in *Ma Griffe*, which is always such a comfort, and then I went down to the bar to meet Peter, as we had arranged. It was a pleasant bar, not one of those fearful ritzy things all mirrors and Maraschino cherries, but an authentic bar where the locals come; all worm-eaten oak and uncleaned pewter, and tankards of beer, and men in mended jodhpurs and riding mackintoshes talking about fishing. I was awfully glad that I hadn't changed because I felt that I blended in fairly non-committally, if you know what I mean.'

'It sounds quite a strain, all this blending in.'

'I *was* beginning to feel a bit shivery inside, because I hadn't any status and I'm not the casual week-ender type. So I ordered myself a brandy and soda, as Peter hadn't turned up yet, and I somehow felt the brandy was a trifle out of keeping. I ought to have quaffed a pint of porter, or something like that, except that it might have made me throw up, and that would have been more than conspicuous. Then I bought half of mild for the village girl who served behind the bar, and she seemed to accept me as *bona fide*, which made me feel very fraudish, but I had enough sense to smile sweetly and fold my hands, as though nothing were out of place. Then when the fishing men moved off, we were left together, the barmaid and I, and after she'd gulped the second half of mild, and I'd ordered another brandy, she told me I'd missed the excitement. They'd had a real film star, all glitter and stuck-on eyelashes, and the deepest-cut Dior anyone in those parts had ever seen. That cheered me up no end, because I felt that after the film star no one would notice me, not being, in any event, a noticeable type.'

'Peter seems to have the knack of disappearing, doesn't he?'

'When he did arrive at last, I'd almost forgotten about him, having, as it were, merged myself perfectly into the background by then. I suppose I must have looked a trifle surprised to see him, because he got quite huffy about it, and said Didn't I expect him, and I said, Yes, I'd expected him half an hour or so ago, but somehow he'd gone out of my mind since. You know how one does say such awful things when, caught off one's guard, the truth pops out? Then he had the grace to apologize for being late, but he'd thought I'd be hours and hours, and he was just checking up on the tyres or pressure, or something. Evidently in spite of the old-world atmosphere there were all the most up-to-date gadgets secreted in some shed in the courtyard, and Peter just couldn't resist taking the car's temperature, and so on.

'After a wonderful dinner, venison and cheese soufflés and peaches, and coffee, and more brandy, I felt much restored. But *still* I didn't know where I was, if you know what I mean.'

'Didn't Peter give you any clue?' I asked.

'Not a morsel, that was the most maddening thing. I began

to feel that I'd made a big mistake, and he'd whip out his Leica and all his box of tricks of lenses and lights and tripods, and what not, and start photographing everything furiously, and perhaps that was what he really *had* come for. It puts one in such a false position not to know what position one is supposed to be in, and not to have the remotest idea of what line to take. After dinner we went upstairs to the drawing room, which was all satin and looped curtains and little glass tables with bibelots inside them, all very exquisite and unusual. And I realized I'd been brought somewhere terribly special, but if only the whys and wherefores could have been made a bit plainer. We had the room to ourselves, too, which to anyone having an illicit weekend ought to have been heaven – if they knew, that is, that they were having an illicit weekend. It just made Peter one mass of nervous jitters. He kept on walking around the room and clearing his throat and making futile comments on the furniture. Then he picked up a tiny paper knife, circa nineteen-ten, I should think, and *ugly*, and stared at it so long and so seriously I thought I should scream.'

'I think you showed great self-control,' I said. 'Although maybe it would have been better if you *had* screamed.'

'I just sat there, remembering my room, and the fire wasting itself away, and the writing desk by the window, which looked as though it might have belonged to Anne Hathaway, and I began to wish that I could go back there, and be all quiet and peaceful by myself, and pretend that I was living hundreds of years ago. I tried to think what I could write sitting at the desk, but I couldn't think of a thing, which was such a pity. I knew I'd tell you all about it so there wasn't much point in writing, and I couldn't very well write to my aunt in Tunbridge Wells and say that I was spending a weekend with a young man in an enchanting inn, could I?'

I said no, she might have been perturbed.

'Besides, the dinner must have been fabulously expensive,' said Alexandra, 'and I think Peter spends all his spare money on that cosseted car of his, so I couldn't imagine that he'd let himself in for all that just for company. Anyway, he hummed and hawed and wandered about absolutely relentlessly, and the strain was nearly intolerable. Even he seemed to feel the thickening of the atmosphere, and we were both almost gasping for breath by that time. Then he said he must go and check up if the car was all right, and, enigmatically, that he would see me later.'

'Did he say where he would see you?' I asked.

'No, so for ages I just stayed put, until I got sick to death of it, and I went back to my own room and threw another bit of tree on the fire, and sat down at the desk and looked out of the window, but it was very dark and leafy, and anyway my window faced the front, so I couldn't see if Peter was pacing the courtyard or not. It was all most peculiar. Then I crashed my way to the lavatory, which was as difficult to find as the centre of any maze, and worse because of all the little drifts of steps going up and down, and passages that suddenly narrowed and ended in windows, and so on. There seemed to be only about five bedrooms, and all, I expect, as big as whole houses, like mine was, and if only there had been a couple more bathrooms and quite a lot more lavatories, and the passages hadn't been so fearfully murky, it would have been quite perfect. On the way back I looked into the drawing room, but it was in complete darkness, and by the time I got to my room I felt all weak at the knees, and tired as tired. I waited and waited, hardly daring to undress, in case Peter came back when I was in the middle of it, and I should feel such a fool. Besides one certainly isn't at one's best half dressed, and then I was longing to have a kind of shower bath and to stand in the ewer, but that might have been even more awkward, and there didn't seem to be any means of locking the door. The whole place was too well-bred for that. After about an hour, which seemed half a lifetime, I thought, to hell with this, and I undressed and washed and creamed my face, and pinned up my hair, and I thought if he comes now it will serve him right.'

'Did you mind much?' I asked.

'Not by then. I'd have been more than enthusiastic after dinner, and might have thrown myself into bed with cries of joy, but I'd got past it – long past it. And I slept like the dead, but really, and I might have been sleeping there still, if an elderly maidservant with very bad feet hadn't brought me my breakfast in bed. And the heaven of it – I simply can't tell you. Coffee smelling and tasting exactly as coffee should, and rolls and butter, and stewed figs, just like one used to have years ago. And all willow pattern with gilded edges, and real silver teaspoons, and a tiny linen napkin, hand-embroidered, believe it or not. And the maidservant was very friendly, and said that if it wasn't for her feet it was a lovely morning, bright and crisp, and pretty up the river way, but icy, and I'd have to be careful if we were going up there, as she expected we would. She sounded so certain we were, that it seemed as if up by the river way was what people came for, and it would look very peculiar if we'd come for anything else. So I said Yes, I was almost sure we were, and then she asked whether we'd be needing a picnic basket, which put me in rather a spot, and I said I'd see and let her know soon, and she smiled and hobbled off, apparently quite satisfied. So I ate absolutely every crumb on the tray, and drank every drop of coffee, just as though I'd starved for weeks, and then there was all the business of lifting the hot-water jugs and washing and dressing and looking for the lavatory.'

I said I thought candlelight and pewter and old oak were all very attractive, but a private bathroom might be even more so.

'Especially,' said Alexandra, 'in such peculiar circumstances. On the way back I met Peter, muffled up in a dressing gown, clumpy and camel-haired, and sneezing, and looking cross beyond speech. But I thought, well, it *is* horrid to meet someone who's comparatively pulled together and dressed, when one's still soggy with sleep, and sordid and unshaved. So I just said, "Hallo, darling", in a soft soothing voice, and looked down at my feet, trying to show that I was more than sympathetic, and he muttered something about being along later, then he buried the whole of his face in the largest handkerchief I've ever seen and sneezed fit to blow his head off, and threw himself into the bathroom. And I thought, well, that's a nice thing. He's going to be ill. I went back to my room and packed what little I had to pack, because I didn't know whether we were supposed to be staying there or not. It was preposterous. Then I waited again, and began to get more than sick of it all because the sun was shining, and I thought even in those heels I might manage to totter a few steps and get a breath of air, when, at last, Peter arrived.

'He looked better, but then, of course, he was dressed and shaved, which makes a remarkable difference, but he was a bit peaky, except around the nose where he was pink, and he said he thought he'd caught a filthy cold, and he wanted to get out of the damned place, quick as quick, and when we were in the car he'd tell me about it. I was hustled into the car almost before I knew what was happening, and Peter crashed the gears madly, and seemed in a foul temper, and

I began to wish I'd never begun on the miserable business. I felt frustrated and ill-used and that I had been made a fool of, and heaven knows what else. Except, of course, I might have made a fool of myself, which was even worse to contemplate.'

When she was telling this last part her eyes looked tearful, and I began to feel good and angry with Peter, who seemed to be little, if any, use to any woman, and I did feel that he ought to have made this quite quite clear.

She was silent then, and I saw that she was crying, but only a little, in a most controlled manner; one tear spilled over and she licked it up, very neatly, as it was on its way down, with the tip of her tongue.

'At the risk of continuing to sound like your aunt in Tunbridge Wells,' I said, 'I really can't help saying, once again, that I feel it may all be for the best. I suppose it went on more or less as it began, null and void?'

She managed to smile.

'Yes,' she said. 'Null and void, that's just about it. I suppose I've reached an age when I want more than the going and I have an end in view. Besides, the whole thing became more and more like some second-rate farce, you know, lots of bedroom scenes, and no one actually does anything, which in a farce may be all very well but in real life it's awfully lowering. Evidently Peter really did go and say goodnight to his car, believe it or not, but if you saw Peter and that car together you would believe it. He dotes on the thing, and he's always buying it presents. He's even got a special nightshirt for it, if ever it sleeps away from home – I gather his own garage is the last word in car comfort – but he forgot to put the nightshirt in the boot, and that's why it had to suffer the humiliation of being wrapped up in a common piece of sacking. And that's why Peter went to say goodnight to it, to make sure it wasn't feeling the shame of the sacking too deeply, and that it would survive until the morning. Then he found himself imprisoned in the garage because, of course, he had shut the door behind him, not to let the night air in – that car seems to be a poor frail thing – and it was the kind of door that slides over, and it got slightly out of groove, or something technical, and he couldn't get it open. By then it was very late, and no one else was crazy enough to go and say goodnight to a car, and although he rattled and banged about quite a bit, no one heard, as the garages were right across the courtyard and down a little lane. Of course, he didn't want to create a fearful commotion by hallooing for help, and even if he had it wasn't likely that anyone would have heard. Or they'd probably have thought it was a fox or some other weird country noise. What was so utterly unfair was that he seemed to blame me for not coming to *look* for him. But, as I tried to explain, how could one do it? Just imagine me tottering over those cobblestones, looking for the young man who might, or might not, have wanted to make a dishonest woman of me. He seemed to think that I ought to have had premonitions about him, that I ought to have been able to nose him out, as it were. But, as I told him, supposing I had, I can't see myself getting a door back in its groove, and I'd have had to knock up the whole hotel, and that would have been jolly, wouldn't it?'

'Did he have to stay there all night, then?' I rather enjoyed the idea of that. It seemed to have more justice in it than one usually expects to find.

'As far as I can make out only an hour or two. He said he gave up once, and just sat in the car and tried to sleep, but he got chilled to the bone and had one last shot, and the door slid back, easy as easy, as though it had never stuck.

So, boiling with rage against me, he just upped and went to bed. A good job he did, on the whole, because by then I couldn't have cared less, being covered with cold cream and fast asleep. We had a silent drive homewards, only stopping for meals, but by the late afternoon it was obvious that Peter was simply in no condition to go on, and I can't drive: he had a streaming cold, and kept on taking both hands off the steering wheel to sneeze, which wasn't exactly a pleasant sensation for me. So we stopped just outside Oxford for the night, and I thought at least I'll know where I am this time, and no monkey business. Anyway Peter had a temperature and took to his bed straight away, and clearly wasn't fit for anything. I had dinner in solitary state, not very gay, and I let myself be picked up, quite commonly, in the hotel lounge afterwards. But only because I was so miserable and felt grateful. It was only an *en passant* hour, and the man wasn't even staying in the hotel, just there for the odd drink, and to see if anything was doing, and there was only me – not a great deal of choice. And although he was awfully complimentary, and stared as though he couldn't take his eyes off me, ever, I wasn't much moved, and I went off to bed, early, and alone. I think my pick-up was a bit dashed. He seemed to think the nights were free-for-all, which I thought was a trifle too swift, even for me in my lowered state. I mean he hadn't even bought me dinner. Don't you think that was a bit much?'

I said yes, I thought that was rushing things.

The recorder had stopped ages ago, and there was a deep and sinister silence from Pisa's room, and I rather wanted to snoop outside and to listen, which I would not have liked to admit to Alexandra, being, I realized, very unworthy. But as Alexandra was, by then, busily sorting through old gramophone records, choosing mostly sad little French songs of years ago, all ready for a session of sweet remembrance, I was able to absent myself for a while.

I hovered for a few seconds outside Pisa's door, feeling rather mean, but I knew little about her, and all those pricks on her arm were not exactly reassuring. Then I heard Marius talking in impassioned tones about a new dish which he had concocted for Mummy, and how he fried the shallots very lightly in butter, then added the lettuce and half a pint of white wine – so I tiptoed off much ashamed of myself.

We heard Pisa and Marius in the passage, and there was a certain amount of girlish giggles and a little playful scuffling before she let him out.

Then Pisa came in to bid us goodnight, and to thank me, prettily, for letting Marius come to see her. She looked very fetching in a green silk skirt and a black pullover; her hair was braided with green ribbon. And I thought how well she presented herself, at the top of her form every time.

'I notice that Marius kept well away from us,' said Alexandra. 'He ought to be ashamed of himself, falling for Pisa, and at his age, too. Don't you think so?'

'I haven't really thought about it, and, anyway, does it matter?'

Rather sulkily, Alexandra said that she supposed it didn't but it was the principle of the thing. Then she said she was tired and took herself off, leaving me to put away the gramophone records.

A great yawn welled up inside me when I remembered all the confidences which I had listened to, and the advice which I had proffered, during the past few years – none of which, doubtless, had been either acceptable or accepted. Having little direct life of my own, I had been glad to live, second hand, through other people. Yet it was often enervating, too, and I thought what a nice change it might be to have a modicum of direct experience.

I remembered those who had come and gone, and one who had died, and I began to wonder how the years had passed so quickly and left so little trace.

And now to snatch at the butt-ends, as personified, for instance, by Donald: a very worthy young man, no doubt, but of no possible interest to me. Why had I agreed to go and hear Schubert with him in the Town Hall, of all places, on Wednesday evening? Why? I would have been better off with Bernhardt, whom I had churlishly refused.

All of which made me feel that I had better keep my mouth shut. What right had I to give advice, when I had messed up my own life so thoroughly? And not only that, when I was more than capable of continuing to mess it up.

I kept on thinking about Donald – and the Town Hall. Together, they reduced my very being to a state of negation; as if the core of me had been cancelled out.

The telephone rang. It was Donald, to remind me about Wednesday evening. I heard myself saying, with great enthusiasm, how much I was looking forward to it – which depressed me further.

I decided that no good would come of the rest of the day, and I had better go to bed. And once in bed I began to think about Alexandra, and to wish I could find her a perfectly suitable husband. I could see him, in my mind's eye, wearing his bowler hat to the manner born.

Then, as often before, I dreamed myself to sleep with remembrances of a summer life in the country: the scent of grass, new-cut, and warm, soft-aired evenings; watering and clipping and planning for the future – a future which has already gone. The hot, bright mornings, spent weeding the strawberry beds, picking raspberries, tasting the summer all the time, every hour of the day. Being part of a garden, part of a wood, part of a meadow; part of all the thriving busyness around, of growth and decay, and building up to begin again.

Then there were the small, light, flower-filled rooms, and such a sense of peace there; such a sense of being cast off, unget-at-able. And yet I knew it was impractical to wish time back. I knew, too, that I needed the life of a city. But if only I could have a few hours back again; the very ordinary hours; to hear once more the dawn chorus of birds, the birds of one's own garden, lovely and commonplace and unforgettable; to sit on the terrace in the early mornings; to hear the trains breaking the deep silences of the night; to pick apples and to dig one's own potatoes. To remember, inevitably, only the best of it all – the sun-hazed, soft-aired summers of years ago. To discard November fogs, and winter's dreariness, and the sad forsaken months of a year's beginning. To bring only the best to mind. And so to sleep, serenely.

The next two days I spent typing the novel at the rate of about twelve thousand words a day, which was just about all I could stand. And still I had only reached the halfway mark. It was inordinately long.

The cheque for the ceramics arrived, followed hard upon by the electricity bill which, as usual, was twice what I had expected.

Pisa said she would like to pay for her room, if I would allow her to stay; she had some nebulous scheme for visiting people's houses and doing oddments of sewing and alterations.

When I asked her whether she was really good at that sort of thing she hedged a bit, and said that she had many ideas. Even she seemed doubtful how they would turn out in practice.

She said she would babysit, exercise dogs, go in when people were away and feed and talk to their cats, and attend to their plants; all in all, she was prepared to be both useful and companionable for seven shillings and sixpence an hour, and for dog-exercising, cat-feeding, and plant care she would charge less. It sounded somewhat dotty, but she seemed intent upon trying it out.

'I do it all private, on the side,' she said. 'Pay no tax. I am registered as student, and no one will find out.'

'Now look here, Pisa.' I put on my sternest manner. 'You can do what you please, and it's no affair of mine, but I don't want to know how you propose to diddle the income tax. For one thing you probably *will* be found out – and don't ask me how, but they seem to have sinister ways and means – and for another the less I'm told the happier I shall be. And for heaven's sake don't leave me to cope with Inspectors of Taxes or National Insurance officials, asking why you haven't paid this, that or the other. You'll most likely be out, exercising Mrs Vassenheimer's animals, or watering someone's plants, and I shall be left to face some angry government department. That I will not stand for.'

Pisa laughed, merrily. 'No,' she said, 'Pisa would not do that to you. All my friends pay no taxes.'

'So they may,' I said, 'and you'll probably all be thrown into jail at the same time.'

If the electricity account hadn't arrived that very morning, I would probably have turned down Pisa's suggestion. As it was, I felt there was something to be said for it.

'But, Pisa,' I warned her, 'I simply must have peace of mind. I can't spend my time worrying what you are getting up to.

And if there's any chance of your wanting urgently to get up to something, then for heaven's sake don't stay on here.'

Pisa considered this rather glumly. Then she came to a decision. 'Pisa will behave perfectly.' Then added, frankly: 'Anyway, Pisa damn broke and will have to work hard.'

'We're all damn broke,' I said, 'and somehow one can never seem to work hard enough to catch up.'

Pisa promised that she would do her own room, and that she would cheerfully undertake any small jobs which I might want done; that she would make herself generally useful. It sounded all right.

I began to try to ferret it all out financially. At least what Pisa paid would enable me to have Mrs Aitch once or twice a week to do the 'rough'; all the things which one doesn't want to have to do oneself – which usually means that they don't get done. After the first few times Mrs Aitch would no doubt talk herself out, which might be a blessing. As for Pisa, it would be pleasant, in many ways, to know that somebody else was in the flat, although I rather hoped that I would not have too overpowering a knowledge of Pisa's presence.

The next evening, before going off to meet Donald, I told Alexandra about Pisa's staying in the flat, and asked her what she thought about it.

'Yes, I can see there's quite a lot to be said for it.' She sounded dubious. 'And you can always give her the push, can't you? I mean if she gets too rollicking.'

I said it was a pity Pisa wouldn't be out all day, because it might be a bit tiresome having someone popping in and stewing up this or that, and then popping off again to mend someone's linen or dog-sit, or whatever it was she contemplated doing.

'That will be a bit of a bind,' said Alexandra. 'One will

never know whether she's there or not. I wouldn't like it myself, but then it would be more difficult for me, what with the infants coming at all hours and having to be made much of and given one's absolute attention. I'd hate to know that someone was likely to bounce in asking what she could do, and insisting on being helpful.'

'I must try it now,' I said. 'I did promise I would. Besides, things are even tighter than usual, and I don't fancy living too hard. I'm too old for that.'

'Talking of living hard, I've decided to do that cat book – that is if the offer's still going. So don't be surprised if you see me struggling with a basketful of cats, will you? I expect they'll all be Siamese and howl and scream like devils, and I shall be turned out for causing a public nuisance. I've tried to do some sketches of the cat next door, that awful old ginger creature with half an ear, but they haven't really come off. I feel that I must have a cat which has *joie de vivre* and a personality. The ginger just waits to be let out, and then waits to be let in; it's got that flat-faced, deadpan look of the over-domestic animal. But perhaps there's nothing between that and the wild ones that leap all over the place and claw madly at everything? Anyway, if I get it, it'll be £50 on signature of contract, or on publication date if I'm unlucky, and seven and a half per cent. And that's not to be thrown over lightly, is it?'

I said one just didn't know what to do for the best.

Then she told me that a friend of Peter's had written one of those mountain-climbing books, and in spite of all the mountains that had been climbed it did not occur to him that he might not be able to get it published, and he wanted it typed, as quickly as possible, and would I like to do it?

I leapt at the chance, having, apart from the novel, come to the end of my 'orders'.

'He seems to have plenty of money,' said Alexandra, 'and he wants to give his book a good start, and the best of everything; thick paper and properly sewn together afterwards. So you can charge your top prices.'

I said it sounded wonderful, and then remembered I was meeting Donald, and that I would have to get myself ready.

'I do hope you don't mind,' I said. 'But I think he wants me to be a mother to him. He's probably regretting it sadly by now, anyway.'

Alexandra assured me that she didn't mind in the least, and all she hoped was that *I* didn't object to being landed with a bus conductor as the result of her party.

'As a matter of fact,' she warned me, 'you may find him a bit heavy on the mind, if you know what I mean. He will insist on burdensome discussions on a rather elementary intellectual level. And even those I find difficult to keep up with. I expect he wants to improve himself.'

I said I was afraid she was right.

I met Donald at the Town Hall, as we had arranged. He looked very clean and neat, and neither pleased nor displeased, merely purposefully intent on being seated well before the concert was to begin.

As he had paid for the tickets, I felt in honour and age bound to ask him back to my flat for coffee and sandwiches afterwards.

He accepted, without much enthusiasm. I believe he *had* begun to wonder why he had invited me.

I looked around, somewhat nervously, for Bernhardt, and felt thankful that he was nowhere to be seen. I realized that Donald was a serious listener; and supposing we were joined by Bernhardt there would probably be a commotion of talk, because Bernhardt would be sure to comment and to criticize. Donald would not relish that.

The Schubert came first, and was to my ears all that music ought to be. After the interval there was something very loud, merely called Variations, by someone I had never heard of. Also it was very long, or perhaps I was not capable of listening any more. I suppose I must have fidgeted a bit, and Donald gave me one or two hooded glances of distaste. My reactions were not what he required. He resented me.

When the concert was over I said I was sorry, but the piece after the interval just wasn't my kind. In fact I found it positively hurtful to my ears.

'You ought to have something done about it,' he said meaningfully, with semi-controlled wrath. 'Fancy not being able to listen to such a stereotyped work. Its form is perfectly classical. If you like music at all, then you ought to be able to appreciate that.'

I replied, meekly, that I found it awfully loud.

Feeling, perhaps, that he ought to get even with me for the music's sake, he pointed out a remarkably pretty young woman with whom, he gave me to understand, his relations had been very intimate indeed.

I asked him how he had lost her, and he said, rather loftily, that he had done nothing of the kind. They had both decided that they were not suited to a bourgeois suburban existence. That shook me, as I had not realized that people still said such things.

'Besides,' he added, 'I want to get on, and a fat chance I'd have with a wife and kids hanging round my neck. Women don't believe in education, they don't want you to get on, at least not once they're married. All they want's a home and to go out to the pictures, or look at television, and to buy themselves new clothes.'

I said I was sorry to hear it.

'It stands to reason,' he said, 'all women's ideas change when they get married.'

I replied, coldly, that he must have had the misfortune to have found himself surrounded by a great quantity of moronic females, and we walked back to my flat in an atmosphere of silent discomfort.

After I had produced sandwiches and made coffee Donald thawed somewhat, as he was a firm believer in paying for his supper with stimulating conversation.

Apparently he was a member of several obscure sects, all of which were intent upon putting the world to rights. He told me at great length exactly why he thought war was a bad thing; I doubt whether it had occurred to him that anyone else had ever reached this conclusion.

I asked him about his shorthand and typing, but he was in no mood to consider such practicalities.

I realized that his meek and mild behaviour at Alexandra's party was his first-encounter manner; what he really wanted to do was to lay down the law, and in the intervals to pick up what crumbs of knowledge he could. Not that I cared; I was perfectly prepared to be bowled over by his eloquence, if that gave him pleasure. But I felt sorry that he should have chosen me; there was little, if anything, which he could learn. I had neither the interest nor the capacity.

After his second cup of coffee he asked me what I thought of Christopher Fry, Anouilh, Seton Merriman and Thomas Hardy – as ill-assorted and confusing a quartette as I have ever tried to deal with.

He listened politely, and then swept my words aside by

saying that, from the little he'd read so far, he didn't think much of any of them, but they came into his programme of study for the winter. I said that ought to keep him busy, and then I yawned long and openly, until Donald realized what was expected of him and said he thought he ought to go.

It was quite a few minutes before I could manoeuvre him towards the door, so that he could translate his suggestion into action. As he was on the point of departure, Pisa glided out of her room, followed by one of the lesser Peters, who looked a bit ashamed of himself, and I hoped with no definite reason. Pisa automatically flipped her braided hair, opened her eyes widely at Donald, and greeted him prettily, reminding him that they had met at the party, and Donald muttered something that sounded like, 'Coo, could he ever forget such a good-looker?' Then he turned away, blushing hotly, obviously sick of himself for allowing such words to escape.

But Pisa didn't mind a bit. To her a compliment was a compliment, and the phrasing was immaterial.

'Poo,' she said, entering into the spirit of the thing, 'I am not all that pretty, no?'

The lesser Peter was getting all hot and damp around the collar, and no wonder.

I said, rather sharply, that they must either get themselves out, or, if they wanted to make a night of it, but I hoped not too much of a night, they had better take themselves back to Pisa's room, and would Pisa *please* remember to lock up.

I felt sorry for the lesser Peter, and I tried to throw him a bone of sympathy, to show that I knew he had been caught up, willy-nilly, and he wasn't by nature a hanger-about in hallways.

In return he managed a half-smile in my direction, pallid

and placating, and then shot out of the front door like a rabbit.

Donald followed, somewhat quicker than he had intended, helped by a small push from me.

I locked up, and Pisa, rather cast down, offered to wash my coffee cups with her own. Which offer I accepted gratefully.

I realized again that there would be lots of snags in having Pisa around; always colliding with her and some follower was one of the worst. I wondered whether she would consider it too undignified if I suggested, for the sake of both our private lives, that she and her friends should use the back door. She could even have a little card with her name on it outside the door, if she wished – although the landlord mightn't care for that. But supposing she did use the back door, she and whoever else was with her would be leaning around in the kitchen saying interminable good nights locked together between the refrigerator and the cooker, and one would never be able to get to anything without coming upon them.

Certainly it was a problem.

Later that same week Alexandra saw the publisher of the cat book.

'He's really quite ordinary,' she said, 'and not a bit propositioning. At least he wasn't to me. But perhaps I'm not his type. And I'd mugged up one or two frightfully dignified sentences, all ready for the occasion. As the occasion didn't come about, and I was left with a perfectly proper and disinterested publisher on my hands, who didn't even leer once, I was rather at a loss. I stood there, all dumb and silly. Anyway he says he thinks I can do what he wants, from what he's seen of my work. He says he thinks I have an insight into the child mind – I wasn't too keen on the way he put it. But I'm in no position to get all upstage, so I just smiled and said I'd do my best. I'm to do a few roughs for him first, and he's going to send along the cat model this afternoon. There's glory for you. It's the story of a particular cat, so that it must be that cat, and no other. It sounds a bit gaga to me, but who am I to start arguing? Even if he doesn't like the roughs, he'll pay me a guinea or two, to show willing, as it were. On the whole, he's behaving most British, don't you think?'

I must have been out, or typing, or perhaps just dozing, because I neither saw nor heard the cat's arrival. Instead of coming down to visit me that evening, Alexandra telephoned to ask me to go up.

'I do want you to come and look at this cat,' she said. 'His name's Tom, and he just won't cooperate.'

When I arrived I found Alexandra looking wild and windswept; the cat looked remarkably tame and lethargic. He was lying in front of the electric fire, fast asleep.

We stood and stared down at him. He was a very large cat, black and white; he had a very large black-and-white face, and extremely long light-grey whiskers.

'How did he come?' I asked. He was obviously such a self-possessed cat that I could imagine him arriving carrying a little suitcase and ringing the front doorbell.

She pointed to an outsize in cat baskets. 'Tucked up in that,' she said. 'In a cab. He had already been paid for, and well tipped for, I should say. The taxi man was most affable. Tom brought his own box, too, full of some frightfully special non-stinking stuff. The box is on the balcony. He knows it's there, I think. But I couldn't even prod him awake long enough to show him properly. Not that he cares, anyway. He only wants to sleep. I've sketched him from all angles asleep, and what they want to see is *action*. I've tried him with everything; cotton reels, and screwed-up bits of crackly paper, and saucers of cream, and all that cats are supposed to dote upon. He just sleeps through. He did open an eye for a couple of seconds, and actually began to lick one of his paws, but even before I'd grabbed a pencil the effort was too much for him, and he sank back exhausted. I've never seen such a cat.'

'Supposing I picked him up?' I suggested somewhat timidly. I've never known a cat intimately. 'Do you think he'd turn savage?'

'Not a hope,' she said. 'I've held him at all angles, practically upside down, and he just sleeps. It isn't natural. Why, that miserable ginger next door is dynamic compared to Tom.'

'Perhaps he's too well fed,' I suggested. 'If you can keep him for a few days and cut his rations down, he might get a bit alert.'

We watched him for a while, but still he slept, and slept all curled up and creased, so that he didn't even look much like a cat; just a rolled-up bit of fur.

'He's obviously a remarkably fine specimen,' I said. 'Probably a king of cats, but he doesn't seem to have much interest in life.'

The whole time I was there Tom didn't move. Even when I tickled him under the chin he made no acknowledgment; he didn't even stretch or show the slightest sign of animation.

The next evening Alexandra arrived wearing the still dozing cat around her neck. 'You don't mind, do you?' she asked. 'I thought a change of scene might do him good.' She sat down and the cat collapsed in her lap, in exactly the same position as he had lain the previous evening, and fell fast asleep immediately.

'He sits down to eat,' she said, almost in awe. 'When he wants to go to his box he just opens his eyes and stares at the balcony door, and when he seems to be going into a trance again I haul him up and carry him out. He scratches around and performs, and then just waits to be brought back.'

'Doesn't he rush around at night when *you* want to go to sleep?' I asked. 'He looks the sort of perverse cat that might bide his time.'

'Nothing like that. I don't believe he knows he's a cat. I don't believe he knows what he is. He's just a thing. He's probably some very rare missing link in cats; he hasn't evolved yet, or whatever it's called. When I switched off the electric fire just before going to bed last night any self-respecting cat would have looked cross, but he just went on lying in front of a fire which wasn't on. So I went to bed and left him. But somehow I kept on thinking of that wretched cat getting colder and colder, and waking up with rheumatism, or cat flu, or whatever cats do get, so I got up and fetched him, and he slept on my feet underneath the eiderdown. Today I was so desperate I cheated a bit, and did some sketches of that mangy old ginger next door and put Tom's face on them. Of course, the ginger isn't exactly lithesome, but he does stroll down the garden now and again.'

'Has Tom got a special kind of cat face?' I asked, trying to contort myself and look upside down to get some idea of what he was like. Seen full on, from the snug way in which he was lying, he did not appear to have a face at all.

'As a matter of fact he has. He's got a quite definite cat face. There's nothing wrong with him physically. He's a perfect creature. It's his brain that's gone, or maybe he hasn't ever had one. Perhaps he doesn't coordinate.'

The next day Alexandra went off and bought Tom a toy

mouse; it was made from a scrap of mouselike fur and had a thin rubber tail. It was too real to be nice.

'That ought to get him,' she said. 'He must have some inherited instincts, even if he's never actually come in contact with a mouse before.'

I accompanied her upstairs to watch Tom's expression – if any. He opened his eyes, just, when Alexandra dangled the mouse on his whiskers. He glanced up pityingly at her, and sighed. Then he put out one paw in an almost catlike gesture, gathered the mouse to his bosom, curled himself around it, and snuggled down again. We could not even see the mouse, let alone Tom's face, which was entirely hidden.

'Poor thing,' said Alexandra. 'He's suffering from a kind of repressed mothering instinct. But perhaps when he wakes up and finds he's got something of his own to look after, that will give him just the incentive he needs.'

When Tom did wake up he shook himself free of the mouse, and then went back to sleep in his original position.

'I think I'll just have to take him as a symbol,' said Alexandra, 'and concentrate on the ginger. It only goes to show, doesn't it, that when a publisher turns out not to be the propositioning kind he may have something much more awkward up his sleeve.'

Tom had his uses, though; Alexandra told me he made an excellent focus of attention for two particularly difficult children whose portraits she was painting.

'They're twins,' she said, 'so shy they're speechless. They wear their hair in ratty pigtails knotted at the back, and even their hair is no colour. They both wear spectacles, and they both have braces on their teeth, not that they can help that. But it took me until the third sitting before I came to, as it were, and suggested they could take off their braces just for the occasion. And they actually smiled, both at once, and looked quite transfigured. Tom was a wonderful help. They sat together and nursed him between them. They're so thin and leggy that they look like the children one sees in *Punch* drawings about nineteen-hundred. I've actually painted Tom in the portrait; he seems to make a link between them, as a bit of him is on one lap and a bit on the other. I don't suppose an animal is copyright, or anything like that, do you?'

I said no, I didn't think so.

Then I told her that Pisa had been bouncing about a bit, and seemed to have lots of followers, which was rather disturbing from the practical point of view of sensing that the flat was full of people, even if I never actually met them.

'Oh yes, I do see,' she said. 'But I expect she's just feeling her first waft of freedom, and she'll settle down and pick and choose later. I think in spite of all that waggle-waggle she's really hardly at all sexy. Probably less than we are, and heaven knows no one would think that of us, would they? Quite likely she's really what Marius said, "a nice unassuming gairl", or something like that, but she can't help curving about and swaying more than somewhat – it's just her type. And then, of course, going in so at the waist means that one has to come out above and below, which makes it all the more noticeable, doesn't it? I don't think Marius would be so keen, and he must be somewhat because he keeps on dragging in her name whenever we meet, if she wasn't, *au fond*, fairly unfledged in her desires. If she'd ever made a rush at him, he'd have run screaming. What with Mummy now, and a most peculiar lot of ancestors, Marius is, I should imagine, pretty well drained.'

'What kind of ancestors?' I asked.

'Well now, they're the kind that hang all around the wall; all looking like Marius, but Marius with something added, and I should say they were all depraved in the lowest possible meaning. So Marius, of course, is just the emasculated result of what used to go on.'

'What did go on?' I asked, impatiently.

'There was Marius's grandfather, for instance, who kept on making trips to the East when practically no one got further than Lake Como. That was suspect enough, to start with. He went complete with wife, the wife's friend, a Lady Somebody of dubious reputation – a very handsome woman, I've seen a painting of her – and the grandfather's own special friend, the Honourable George, *and* they acquired whatever took their fancy on the way. And they seem to have had quite a lot of fancies. The story goes that they used to arrive in Mecca, or wherever they were aiming for, complete with a couple of brace of Arab boys, all very young and succulent, and one or two or more Persian slaves, females, willowy and black-eyed, and then they'd really get going and have no end of fun together. Marius's grandfather was supposed to have had an enormous bed especially made for such occasions and shipped out to the villa, or mosque, or palace, or whatever, and they slept together. Not just that, but everyone took turns with everyone else, if you see what I mean. I suppose it must have been quite the top of that kind of thing, if that's the kind of thing one likes. It sounds all rather tiring to me. I wonder if one could ever say "I think I'll sit this round out", but that might have been letting the side down. He, the old man, was nearly in his dotage when he began all this caper, because he had had to wait until *his* father died before he could squander the estate in riotous living – and when people talk about riotous living nowadays, I wonder whether they ever imagine anything quite as riotous as that? So you can hardly wonder that Marius isn't exactly all there, can you? And I don't mean by that what people usually mean.'

'What about Marius's father?' I asked, taking a deep breath. I have a visual mind, and the whole recital had been rather a strain on it.

'Oh, he was more of a watcher than a doer – at least so I've heard. Of course, Mummy must have been odd to marry him, but the story goes that her relations with *her* father were much more and rather different from what they ought to have been.'

'Who would have thought it? And now Marius. Certainly nature has taken her revenge.'

'Not only on Marius,' said Alexandra. 'We all seem to be nature's revenges. It is most unfair. Look at Peter. I suppose Jung or Freud or Adler (or don't they count now?) or some behaviourist could explain exactly why Peter got himself shut in that garage, but whatever the reasons the result is the same as far as I'm concerned. If I don't take care I shall become frustrated. One almost gets to the point when anything male in shape and primeval in purpose will do excellently.'

I considered this rather glumly.

'Talking of that,' said Alexandra, 'I met the man I told you about – the one who picked me up in rather peculiar circumstances in the hotel outside Oxford –'

Suddenly she looked at her wristwatch and said that Marius was calling for her in half an hour, and she must fly.

It was the next day when the snow began to fall; it fell slowly, softly, ceaselessly, then for a few hours it stopped, only to begin again. Overnight the temperature fell suddenly, and the snow which had begun to melt froze over again, covering everything with a thin layer of ice.

I waited to see whether anyone else would sweep the steps and the side path, but in the end I was forced to appeal to Mrs Aitch.

'Lor bless you,' she said. 'O' course I'll come an' clear you out. Why didn't you say? That Mr What's-his-name on the first floor's about as good as a sheep, in't 'e? I only said to Mr Aitch yesterday, there's them two women snowed up as like as not, and 'oo cares?'

Who indeed? I thought, but did not say so, feeling that it would further weaken my position.

When Mrs Aitch had shovelled and swept and put down salt (in which she was a great believer) I told her about Pisa, and asked Mrs Aitch whether she could spare me a few hours regularly each week. She said she could, but added, belligerently: ''Oo's this young woman? Is she the one 'oo wears them 'orrible trousers? Ah, I thought as much. I've seen 'er. Another of them foreigners round these parts, as if we 'aven't got enough already.'

I heard myself saying yes, I was afraid so, and then I wished I hadn't.

'You be careful,' said Mrs Aitch darkly, obviously all set to protect me. 'A friend o' mine was working fer one of them and she cut 'er throat.'

'Who cut whose throat?' I asked.

'The *woman* cut 'er throat.' Mrs Aitch sounded at the end of her patience with me, and I did not pursue the matter. 'You can't trust 'em,' she said. 'Never know what they'll do next.'

I told myself that I ought not to encourage this hobnobbing, and yet heaven knows where I would be if I didn't. Probably snowed up for weeks.

'An' she wasn't no better than she ought to be, if as good,' said Mrs Aitch with menace. '*An*' she was married, and her husband was crippled with something diabolic, and she wasn't never 'ome till two or three in the morning. So I said to my friend, "What does she do staying out half the night?", and my friend says, "She goes dancing". An' I said, "Don't you tell me that for a story – dancing!"'

I felt that we had exhausted the dubious possibilities of Mrs Aitch's friend, and I still didn't know who cut whose throat.

'Dunno why you want ter saddle yourself with a lodger.' Mrs Aitch helped herself to another cigarette. ''Aving someone on yer 'eels the 'ole time. O' course, if you was married that 'ud be different, wouldn't it? Though I've 'ad one man fer twenty-five years an' that's one man too many. Tykes, the 'ole lot of 'em.'

There was a blessed silence for a few seconds. Then Mrs Aitch departed.

Pisa was very happy about the snow, and played around gaily in the little piece of garden, making snowmen of different shapes and sizes. She seemed grateful, though, that she had not been asked to do any shovelling or sweeping.

Mrs Aitch's salt was efficacious; the pathway and the steps to the front door were passable once more.

It was when Pisa and I were in the kitchen that we heard the sound of voices. I knew that it was Alexandra because I recognized the sound of her slim high heels, and because she was wearing the heels she had obviously been out with someone on whom she wanted to make an impression. I remember thinking how silly of her to go out in the snow in such thin shoes.

Pisa craned her head unashamedly and stared out.

'Is mine, is mine,' Pisa cried dramatically, throwing down the tea cloth.

'What is yours?' I asked.

'That man,' said Pisa. '*He* is mine. And because I am not English and do not speak correct, and have no chic clothes, I lose him.'

'I thought men rather fell for the not-speaking-correct routine. And it doesn't matter what you wear – you always look wonderful.' Which was true, but I knew that I did not sound convincing. I felt tired and cross and as though I were getting a cold.

Pisa looked very upset; her mouth drooped and she wiped up several plates which I had not yet washed.

I pulled the tea cloth out of her hands. 'All right, Pisa,' I said. 'I'll finish the washing-up. There isn't much, anyway.'

'It is the same here as other countries,' Pisa wailed, leaning against the draining-board and beginning nervously to scratch the scarlet varnish off her thumbnail. 'Rich, well-dressed, well-spoke, and everyone polite, everyone asks you out. Not me. Pisa has no home, no country, nothing. They only want one thing from me, and that they want free. The foreign men are the worst too. There is that Bernhardt. Here he come all polite, ready to make intellectual conversation. But me, not English, no home, and he push me about all the time, and he treat me like a joke.'

I remembered Bernhardt's behaviour at the party. But then Pisa had apparently enjoyed it all. I decided that I had better not say so. I offered her a cigarette, the inevitable panacea, and then lit one for myself.

'Alexandra isn't rich,' I said, rather against my will, as I felt that there was no point in our discussing Alexandra, and, besides, I ought not to. The trend of the conversation threatened to become emotional, and my instincts were to walk away.

'Maybe not rich, but smooth,' moaned Pisa. 'She did not have to walk from country to country without a home. She has a behaving of being rich. She does not need to wear bright colours and have her hair curled.' Pisa tore the varnish off a fingernail: she had stripped the thumb.

'But you don't have your hair curled, do you?' Pisa's black hair fluffed in tendrils around her forehead; the braided loops began in soft waves at the nape of her neck.

'No, because my hair is curly by itself. If not I would.'

The whole thing was most baffling.

'It is having no safety, like me,' said Pisa, 'which makes misery.' She was silent for a moment, then she smiled. 'I go and lie down and think,' she said. 'And then I paint my nails. You permit?'

'But certainly,' I said. 'You do that.'

I hoped she would have a nice long quiet think.

I finished the washing-up, and then I typed furiously for three hours without a break.

By that time I had nearly finished the novel. It seemed to get longer and longer towards the end; and sadder, too, and much sillier. There was only one woman in it, and she spent most of her life retching and clinging to park railings; and when she wasn't doing that she was leaning her forehead against the wall in some dark alleyway. Leaning her forehead against the wall was to stop her being completely overcome by nausea. I can't remember that it ever did. I wondered how such young men managed to make women feel so sick, so often. And I thought, poor young men, how they suffer.

I could not imagine Pisa, for instance, being reduced to a

state of permanent retching brought about, as far as I could make out, by the writhings of unfulfilled desire. Pisa would complain a little, and then go off and paint her nails a newer brighter pink, then swathe herself in some remnant of gaudier silk, and return, refreshed, to the fray. Alexandra might sniff a little, and even let a tear or two trickle down, but soon she would go off and wash her hair and pour over it an ash-blonde rinse, then either she would put on her 'working' jeans and attack whatever was on the easel or she would dress herself up, finishing off with her highest heels, and totter off, all jaunty, ready for whatever might come along next.

I decided that the young men who wrote novels were better when they wrote about themselves; the ground was firmer for them. I reminded myself, once again, that I did not have to care what it was about – merely to type the wretched thing.

When I was stiff-fingered and numbed practically everywhere else, Pisa knocked at the door. She looked much recovered and renewed after her long think; quite bright and gay.

She was wearing her trews, enormous snowboots, a lumber jacket, a startling green knitted cap with a tiny pompom on the top, and green woolly gloves. Very winter-sports-ish.

'I go now and take out Mrs Vassenheimer's animale,' she said. 'And when I return I have, perhaps, a surprise.'

'Isn't it rather late to take out Mrs Vassenheimer's animale? It will be dark soon.'

'Snow makes everything much more light. I keep him on rein. Besides, it is more excuse.'

I smiled, and said that I quite understood, which I did not.

When she had gone I began to wonder what the surprise could be. I hoped that we were not going to have Operation Water Rats again.

I peeped into Pisa's room. I can well understand now how landladies become what they often do become. Once one begins to count the cost, everything is merely a matter of addition and subtraction.

As I thought, Pisa had gone out leaving the electric fire on. Only one bar, but even so ... If she insisted on staying I would have to get her a separate meter.

Which man could it have been with Alexandra? And why did he belong to Pisa? And what on earth was Pisa talking about?

I forced myself to move; to go and wash, and comb my hair, and make up my face. I looked awful; I hoped it was the mirror, but I knew it wasn't.

There was no doubt about it. I *was* getting a cold.

Before Pisa returned with her surprise, Alexandra flew down the stairs. I knew she was excited by the clatter she made.

'You simply must come up.' She spoke breathlessly, clutching my arm. 'I've got Frederick upstairs. The man I told you about. The man who picked me up, or tried to, in the lounge of the Bear or Bull, or whatever it was, outside Oxford, when Peter was laid low.'

'I'm getting a cold,' I said. 'I could hardly be civil, let alone enthusiastic.'

'You don't have to be enthusiastic – I'm not exactly that myself, just glad that someone's come along to take my mind off Peter. It's like a rest cure. Somebody who cares for me, and I don't care for him.'

I was persuaded, as I knew I should be. I was curious, too, to see the man who used to belong to Pisa, and who had got away.

My first impression of Frederick was that he was extremely

tall. Afterwards I realized that he was middling to tall, but managed to look towering. The immediate sharp impact was that he resembled Tom – a magnificent physical specimen, but whether anything else, I doubted. Time did little, if anything, to efface this doubt.

He had the Viking look: fair-haired, definite bones; greyish blue eyes which looked straight into yours, which I have seldom found necessary, expedient or becoming. I shall never lose the feeling that people who stare frankly at one have much to hide. He had pleasant hands, well shaped, and when he shook hands his grip was perfectly balanced between the friendly and the flabby. He was absolutely everything which one could wish for.

I did not much like him.

Alexandra did not much like him, either. At least that was what I would have said at first, although she was obviously pleased at having landed him, regarding him somewhat as a handsome fish, adept at getting away.

'Wasn't it peculiar,' Alexandra asked, 'meeting Frederick again? I told you about the man in the hotel well, that was Frederick. And then I found him, or, rather, he found me, just outside this very house. It was awfully odd, wasn't it?'

I said, yes, it was indeed odd. And I looked hard at Frederick, and he looked hard back at me.

'It was what I had hoped and hoped for,' he said quietly and modestly, staring in a trance-like way at the carpet.

He told me that he was half Australian (whatever that might mean), and that he had come over here on a grant which he had received from a body called, if I remember rightly, the Australian Universities Incorporated. He was proposing to write a thesis on English literature which was to be linked with English life today.

'Your customs, and your ways, and the general feeling of life in England, which is so superbly old, and gives such a feeling of repose,' he said softly, impressing his quiet strong personality upon us for all he was worth.

I thought of Pisa and Bernhardt and Donald and Mrs Aitch, and Peter hammering on the garage doors in the dead of night, and Marius, and Mummy – especially Mummy – and together or separately they gave me no feeling of repose.

'I think Frederick ought to meet Marius's Mummy, don't you? As an example of old English serenity?'

Alexandra looked reproachfully at me, then suddenly she giggled.

Frederick regarded his hands seriously, and said he would be very glad indeed to meet people, which was what he had hoped for; it would be fine to meet a cross-section of London life.

Then he looked up suddenly and fixed Alexandra with a deep intense stare of definite yearning.

Tom still slept. I thought he was the most reposeful thing I had ever seen.

'This is just the kind of atmosphere I've always wanted,' said Frederick, his eyes still yearningly on Alexandra. 'The atmosphere of a real home, and sitting as we are, in a room like this – and even the cat. For me it is almost too perfect.'

I knew exactly what he meant, and would have agreed, if anyone else but Frederick had said it.

'Actually the cat isn't mine,' Alexandra said practically. 'He's my model for a cat book. Unfortunately he doesn't seem to have the hang of it, and he won't do anything except sleep.'

'He knows where he is well off, and now he can relax,' said Frederick, wistfully. 'May I see some of your drawings? Or don't you like anyone to look at them before they're finished?'

'Of course I do. I'm always longing for people to ask. Somehow they always want to show their own work first, and then there isn't time.' She rose and fetched her sketchbook. 'It's only Tom's face. I had to use the ginger next door for movement.'

Frederick laughed. He had a laugh of such rich sympathy, such genuine charm, that it did not sound true. Every word Alexandra spoke, every movement she made, enchanted him more and more, minute by minute. Alexandra handed the sketches to me first, and I glanced at them fairly casually; they were more or less what one might expect; lightly drawn, pleasantly clean-lined, and, with a bit of pulling together, might be just what was wanted. Then I passed them over to Frederick.

'I think they're quite good,' I said. 'Especially considering Tom's been such a let-down. I like the idea of the *chichi* cat collar with its row of graduated bells. Somehow it gives the cat a definitely aristocratic personality, and makes him *the* cat, not just any cat.'

'I thought you'd spot that. It's a bit of trickery, of course, and although I'm against trickery in principle, sometimes one has to fall for it, to make up for the fact that one isn't actually a genius, doesn't one?'

Frederick certainly wasn't a glancing type; he regarded each rough raptly, concentratedly, narrowing his eyes, holding it away from him, then slowly bringing it towards him, then turning it slightly sideways. All in all his performance took quite a time; for every page received the same intensive treatment.

Alexandra made a small grimace. As we had watched his reactions silently to begin with, we could hardly start to talk then. So we just sat there, waiting for the great god to speak.

At last, in soft, deep, emotional tones, Frederick said:

'They are superb. What excellent movement –' He hesitated, as though overcome.

Alexandra was evidently astounded. Accustomed as she was to a laconic acceptance, a mere nod of recognition, such fulsome praise had overwhelmed her.

'Come, come,' she said, 'that's a bit caddish, isn't it? You needn't be quite so heavily ironic.'

He was gentle and bewildered. 'I assure you,' he said, 'I mean every word. In terms of art I can't express myself technically, but I'm certainly sincere.'

Sincerity oozed from his eyes, and from his fingertips, as he moved his hands in a graceful gesture of amazement.

'Oh, how I believe you!' Alexandra's voice was warm and amused. 'You can go on telling me that for ever and ever. Words of praise – the sweetest music. But of course one can't lap them up immediately, without the least revulsion – just in case. You see, it isn't our kind of thing, Marianne's and mine – we're pretty much down on each other, and if one of us gets uppish the other's ready for the knockout, as it were.'

Frederick frowned, then he let his face go, and he smiled a little, but not too much. All in all, his act was excellently put on – unless, of course, it wasn't put on.

'That is because women are invariably down on each other.' Frederick sounded indulgent.

My doubts rushed back, threefold. Where had I heard that kind of phrase before? Why, from Donald. Of course. Frederick was another Donald, but infinitely better presented; a different background.

'That reminds me of Donald,' I said to Alexandra. She nodded. I think she had caught on.

'Donald? Who is Donald?' Frederick was calm, but intensely watchful.

'A very nice young man whom Alexandra found.' I could not resist teasing him. 'She allowed him to take me out, once, but strictly on loan.'

Alexandra laughed. 'A bus conductor,' she said. 'But quite a pet, and moderately good to look at. Not so good when he opens his mouth, but then one can't have everything.' I thought she regarded Frederick with some regret. Certainly he was better, too, when he did not open his mouth; but in a different way from Donald. Donald was, at least, cleaving a path through, however inexpertly: Frederick was deftly finding his way, which was much worse.

I began to feel that I could not take much more of Frederick, and neither, I was sure, would he choose to take much more of me, and when I was wondering how to make an escape which was not too ungracious the doorbell rang; as I was the nearest, I went to answer it. There stood Marius. He stepped firmly inside, without waiting for an invitation.

Alexandra focused him with a look of sudden guilty remembrance.

'Oh dear,' she said, 'I'm awfully sorry. I didn't go out this afternoon and that's why I forgot that I'd promised to come and see you on the way back.'

'Waiting in a dreary office when everyone's gone home isn't exactly stimulating, so I thought I'd see what had happened.' Marius looked hard at Frederick, immediately realizing that Frederick had happened.

Alexandra introduced them, and Frederick, happily conscious of his physical superiority, and of the fact that because of him Marius had been, at least temporarily, forgotten, made himself behave pleasantly, even if his manner was somewhat patronizing.

There were bleakly uncomfortable pauses in the general

conversation; and it was obvious that Frederick would have preferred Alexandra all to himself.

'I've got to stay,' said Marius, without any of his usual flowery phrases, 'because Mummy's meeting me here so that I can drive her back. I didn't think you'd be busy, Alexandra, as, after all, you did say that you had the evening free and we'd spend it together.'

Alexandra flushed and apologized again, and Frederick glowered.

I noticed that Alexandra was wearing new earrings, blue enamel buttons with tiny patterns of marcasite in the centres. Seeing my glance, Alexandra touched one of the earrings, saying, 'Aren't they pretty? Frederick gave them to me.' Then she held out her hand towards him, and smiled; one of those indescribable half-smiles which a potential lover bestows, and which one feels ought not to have been noticed, being too secret and too private.

Frederick touched her fingers for a second; tight-lipped, Marius looked away.

'Was it awkward leaving Pisa behind?' Alexandra asked, perhaps to break up the uneasy silence.

This possibility I repudiated vehemently. It was just what I did not want to happen, that I should, however indirectly, make myself responsible for Pisa. 'Anyway, she wasn't in.'

I remembered what Pisa had said when Frederick first passed the window. Perhaps he knew that I was connecting him with Pisa in my mind.

'As a matter of fact,' he said diffidently, 'I met Pisa some weeks ago at a party. She seemed lonely, and said she didn't know many people in London. Neither did I as I've just moved up here – I've been boarding a few miles outside Oxford – so I asked her whether she would like to come out some evening.

She gave me her address, and as she wasn't in the telephone book I thought I'd call, on the off-chance, and then, the Lord be praised, I saw Alexandra – since when, I must admit, I haven't been able to take my eyes off her.'

Alexandra babbled on, about how extraordinary it all was, and did not seem to feel that Frederick's all-embracing devotion might suffocate her. She was probably ready to be made breathless; she had had little enough of such pouncing onslaughts.

'Have you anything else especially on hand, apart from the cat book?' I asked, feeling a sudden desperate need of ordinary air.

'Not much,' she admitted sadly. 'I don't know what happens to time. It just slips away.' Then she said that she would make some coffee, and I followed her into the kitchen.

'I suppose it's all right leaving them in there together? Or are they going to begin snarling at each other?' I asked.

'Oh, I don't think so. And even if they do, it doesn't matter much, does it? Unless they're beastly enough to continue after we get back, and I don't think they'd dare, do you?'

I said I didn't know.

'Frederick's morale-building, you must admit, and after Peter – well, I feel I can take a lot of that.'

I nodded: yes, that I could well understand.

'Besides,' she half-whispered, 'I know it oughtn't to count, but when we're out together all the women stare and stare at him, and that's something, isn't it?'

I said yes, it certainly was something, but I still could not understand why they did. He managed to have everything, yet nothing. Not that I could say exactly this to Alexandra, and even if I did she might not know what I meant. I hardly knew myself.

'Perhaps it's his fair hair,' she said; even she sounded a bit puzzled.

'And he has excellent hands,' I added, fatuously, trying, for her sake, to find points in his favour. And yet there were so many.

It was at this moment that Frederick came into the kitchen; tall, easy-striding, his hands in his pockets: 'Break it up, girls,' he said, with a slick camaraderie which did not quite come off. He put his arm casually around Alexandra's shoulders. The gesture, and his words, grated upon me. But who was I to judge? *I* had not been left, deserted, while Peter had tried, unsuccessfully, to find his way out of a garage.

'Your middle-aged admirer in there,' said Frederick with a winning smile, 'seems a bit put out, doesn't he?' Frederick helped himself to a sandwich, ate it in two bites, said that it was good, and put out his hand for another.

Alexandra snatched the plate away. 'You can wait and eat them decently, can't you?'

'Silly little thing,' said Frederick, incapable of believing that whatever he did Alexandra might find displeasing.

I left them to it and went back to join Marius.

'Where did she pick him up?' Marius asked gloomily; he sounded at rock bottom.

'Oh, just sort of found him,' I prevaricated, not knowing how much he already knew.

'Why?' he asked baldly.

'Heaven knows. Except that Peter let her down, or so it seems, and she found this one, who won't let her down in *that* way.'

Marius frowned and blinked his eyes rapidly, which he did when he was upset. 'It isn't that I feel anything like that for her myself,' he said, 'but I wish she'd chosen someone different. I see what you mean about the Peter business, but with Peter it was bound to happen that way, or some way like it.'

I curbed myself asking why it was bound to happen, or, rather, not to happen, with Peter.

'What's this fellow doing over here, anyway?' Marius asked.

I told him all I knew, which wasn't much.

'So he's one of those,' Marius was contemptuous.

'One of what?'

'One of those with grants, and no one knows what for. Second-rate brains. Like mine. Only I haven't got a grant.' He sounded almost on the verge of tears, and his face was quite grey.

'Didn't he tell you about himself?' I asked.

Marius looked shocked. 'We didn't talk,' he said, as though the idea was preposterous. 'We just sat and read the newspapers.'

Then he said he wished I had brought Pisa up, if that was the way Alexandra was going to behave, both of them in the kitchen, kissing or whatever they were doing.

'A thoroughly nice unaffected gairl who makes people happy, and that goes a long way,' said Marius.

I thought I could be nice and make people happy if I looked like Pisa, although I did not say so.

He said that if he'd known Alexandra was going to closet herself away with Frederick, he'd never have said he'd wait for Mummy.

'Where is Mummy?' I asked.

'I don't know where she is at this very minute, but hours ago she said she was going to a tea dance.' He added, bleakly, that she was out with a young naval lieutenant, and wasn't it wonderful how Mummy got them, and at her age, too.

I said, yes, it was more than wonderful. Almost improper. And I didn't realize that there were tea dances nowadays.

He said there must be because Mummy had gone to one.

'Mummy believes in herself,' he said. 'That's the attraction. I have to believe in other people, otherwise I couldn't rewrite their miserable books.'

'I have to type them even before they are rewritten,' I reminded him.

'Why do we do it? You type their illiterate manuscripts, and I revise them, and make suggestions which they haven't even the wit to profit by, then back they come and I sweat over them again. Then they're published and all those morons make themselves reputations, while *we* begin to build somebody else up.'

'Perhaps it is just a question of enthusiasm,' I suggested. 'That's what they've got and we haven't.'

'More impertinence than enthusiasm. Seven semicolons and no verb, and they call that a sentence.'

'But then where would we be without them?'

'Writing our own books, perhaps, and think how much better we'd write them.'

I said he might be, but I wouldn't.

'I've always had a leaning towards the Church,' said Marius. 'But on the bishop level, of course.'

I said yes, of course.

'The trouble with us,' said Marius, 'is that we ought not to be living today at all. I would have preferred the eighteenth century, on the whole. But I think the nineteenth would have suited you better.'

'It wouldn't suit me better now to have been living in the nineteenth century, because I'd be dead, and I'd rather be living, no matter what.'

Marius said I was distressingly literal. 'That's what got Mummy where she is. Looking like something out of the front row of the chorus thirty years ago, yet hard as nails, and horribly up-to-date.'

I said I didn't feel either, and, besides, I hadn't got beautiful legs like Mummy.

He said no, I hadn't, but I was more restful to be with, and that might get me just as far, even if the direction were different.

Just when Alexandra and Frederick returned from their excursion in the kitchen Mummy arrived.

She was swaying a bit, but no more, I imagine, than was customary at that hour in the evening.

Marius immediately looked even more worn; he appeared too old to be Mummy's son, which he knew, and which Mummy knew, and which both resented.

'Aren't I frightful?' Mummy asked coyly, rolling her eyes at Frederick. 'Trailing around after my handsome son? I'm a wicked woman, and I ought to be spanked, that I ought.'

Frederick caught on rather sooner than he should have done, and he went over and sat by Mummy and held her hand. It would not have mattered if he had thrown himself wholeheartedly into the performance; that might have been admirable. But I could not help being repulsed by the way in which he glanced around, when the second was available, to emphasize to Alexandra what a joke Mummy was.

Mummy was working very hard, trying to draw Frederick out. She had been taught to be interested in men, and to ask them questions, because that was what they liked, and she was doing her damnedest, and Frederick, who might have much to hide, was evading her for all he was worth.

Mummy was laughing a lot, and Frederick was pressing

Mummy's hand. He had his arm around Alexandra's waist. I don't think Alexandra was much impressed by Frederick's very sociable manner towards Mummy. Mummy began to care more obviously, and made little feminine clawing gestures at Frederick's lapels with her one free hand.

They all sounded fairly lively and wrapped up in themselves, so Marius and I moved away and sat in the furthest corner.

We listened to Mummy telling a story about Sir Somebody-somebody who had wanted to marry her, but either she was already married or he was, and why he never did marry her when he could have done, and how rich he was. It was all very graphic, with silvery laughter and fluttery gestures.

'It's all nonsense,' said Marius. 'She keeps on making things up. As a family we're finished. We ought to have died off centuries ago, and thank God I'm the last of them. We're perfectly rotten.'

I nodded, although afterwards I realized it was impolite to do so. I ought to have protested.

'Your mother's still remarkably beautiful,' I said, to cheer him up. And so she was; the devil take her.

'Yes,' he said, grimly, 'she's the most beautiful woman I've ever seen in my life.' He was perfectly sincere, but he regarded Mummy with positive hatred. He could forgive her for everything else, but for being the most beautiful woman he had ever seen, never. He did not like men; he would never wholly like any woman; he disliked himself. That was what Mummy had done to him. I wondered whether she would always get away with it, and decided that she would. It would not occur to her otherwise. She was not beset by any fears at all, which made her almost immortal. She may have pondered now and again whether her face would take another lifting, but no more than that.

'Let us hope,' said Marius, 'that Alexandra takes what she wants from that man there, and gets it over with.'

'She isn't that kind,' I said. 'You know she isn't. She's got to have love, and loyalty, and a large firm belief in the future, and all the trimmings.'

'God help her,' said Marius. 'And don't you say a word about this,' he added sharply, looking rather crafty, 'because I shall absolutely deny it. Remember, I'm on their side, anyway.'

'What do you mean, on their side? On whose side?'

'Why, on Alexandra's and Frederick's. The young lovers, and all that. I always make a point of being on their side, otherwise one might be cast off. And it is wonderful to see two young people in love, isn't it?'

I considered this for a moment. 'Thinking it over carefully,' I said, 'I don't find it so at all. If it is pushed in my face then it almost nauseates me. People ought to be able to hold their love, as they ought to be able to hold their drink – to themselves. If we are forced to see that people are either drunk or in love it is embarrassing. It is better not to notice.'

Marius gave a little high-pitched laugh, then he bit off the end of it.

'That is positively subversive,' he said. 'And although, *au fond*, I may agree with you, I'll never admit it. Just remember, I'm on their side, whatever happens.'

'But what will being on their side *do*?'

'Nothing. Except that it means I'm not against them. Which is a lot, as most people will be. Like you.'

'I'm not for or against. Let me make that clear. I want Alexandra to be happy, and Alexandra thinks she won't be happy until she gets married. Perhaps she won't be. I doubt whether Frederick is the ideal husband. That's all.'

'Ah, but then I don't want to lose her, and so I have to keep on Frederick's side, too. It's very tricky.'

'Perhaps you're right,' I said. 'If you are, as you put it, on the side of the young lovers, then it's more likely that it will just fizzle out. Isn't that so?'

Marius looked almost sly. 'That's rather what came to my mind. There won't be anything for them to fight against, will there?'

I began to feel quite respectful. The truth was commonplace, but Marius knew when to use it.

'You're chattering very mysteriously in that corner,' Alexandra called across suddenly. 'What's it all about?'

'Why, us, of course,' Frederick said smugly, embracing both Mummy and Alexandra more affectionately.

'My son's very deep, very deep indeed,' Mummy whimpered. Whatever she had had to drink before she arrived had worn off leaving her sad and unsatisfied.

Marius said he thought it was time they went, and firmly collected Mummy, who kissed me and Alexandra and Frederick, but Frederick longer and more kissingly. Then Alexandra stared meaningfully at Frederick, who said, somewhat reluctantly, that he supposed he ought to go too.

Alexandra said yes, she thought he ought to. And with no good grace Frederick accompanied Mummy and Marius.

The last we saw of Mummy she was tripping down the stairs supported by a cavalier on each side. She looked as though she needed them.

Alexandra yawned.

'Mummy was even more like herself than ever, wasn't she?' Alexandra asked, dully. 'Shall we have a nice, quiet cup of tea?'

I said I thought that would be a good idea, and I went off to make it. There, asleep on the draining-board of all places, was Tom. I made the tea carefully around him so that he should not be disturbed. But as soon as I picked up the tray Tom jumped down and followed me in.

'He takes tea, too,' said Alexandra. 'In the slop basin, with one lump of sugar.'

'Did you really forget all about Marius?' I said, hastily, in case she returned to the recurrent theme of Frederick.

'Absolutely, just as though he didn't exist. By the way, did you manage to get any sandwiches?'

'No, but it didn't matter. I wasn't hungry.'

'I'm afraid Frederick gobbled them all up. He just eats whatever is in front of him.'

While we were sitting and brooding over Frederick there was a soft scrabbling at the door, and Alexandra muttered a few words under her breath before she went to see who it was.

She returned in a few minutes to say that that had been Frederick. He thought he had left his cigarette-case behind.

'Except,' I said, 'that he didn't have one.'

'No,' she said, 'I didn't think he did.'

There I realized, belatedly, that perhaps I ought to have departed.

'Am I cramping your style?' I asked.

'What *do* you think! Not tonight. That's where men have simply no idea, isn't it? Just look at me, practically dying on my feet, and all I want is for Tom to go to his beastly box and come in quick, and in the meantime five minutes' cosy gossip, just the two of us, and he considers he's no end bright coming back for a cigarette-case he didn't even have – and at this time of night.'

'It's downright slovenly,' I said. 'He might have taken the trouble to forget something which he had to start with.'

'*And*,' said Alexandra, 'to risk leaving it behind, even if he'd had to leave his front-door key, and I hadn't opened up, and he'd spent the night in the proverbial gutter. At least that would have shown he cared enough to take a chance. But to come calling at this time of night for a cigarette-case which he never had is asking for quite a lot for nothing, don't you think?'

I said, emphatically, that I did think so.

We sat there, rather solemnly proud of ourselves; two clear-thinking, virtuous women.

'What did you say?' I asked at last. 'How did you get rid of him?'

'I just told him that he didn't bring his cigarette-case, and if he thought that he'd left anything else behind he was wrong, because we had already cleared up, and if there had been anything we should have found it. I was pretty pointed about the whole thing because I remembered that he'd smoked my cigarettes all the evening.'

As I went down the stairs, back to my own flat, I had a snuffle round, but no sign of Frederick lurking about and biding his time. I thought, and hoped, that he had cooked his goose.

The flat was in darkness; Pisa must have gone to bed. I was relieved not to be confronted by Pisa, and her surprise, after all else.

I did not see Pisa until the evening of the next day. After about seven hours' typing I took myself off for a short walk, hoping that that would make me feel better. It didn't.

When I got back Pisa had just returned. She said that she had taken out Mrs Vassenheimer's animale again. She looked pink and glowing and had obviously enjoyed herself no end.

I regarded her with some sour envy. All the lotions and hormone creams in the world could not produce that tint of healthy, youthful flesh, snow-whipped; no eyedrops, nor ice-cold pads, could bring back those clear sparkling eyes; and not even Dior himself, with whatever nippings-in and intricate cutting, could give one that supple, small-waisted figure. But time, I thought, would take it all away; time, and cakes stuffed with banana-flavoured cream. And that was a small, mean consolation.

'My surprise! Please, please, say yes. Say that you do agree!'

'What is it?' I sneezed, shaking myself with the shock. There was no doubt at all. I was getting a cold.

'I am to take out Mrs Vassenheimer's animale, free. She loan me her *ma*chine – you say traddle? One with handle for hands and pedals for feet.'

'Treadle,' I corrected automatically. 'What kind of machine?'

'To sew. I make all my clothes new. I make all yours new. I make everybody's new. Is wonderful. No?'

'Does it need anything special? Does it have to be plugged in?'

Pisa admitted, sadly, that it didn't. 'Is not electric. Is old-fashioned, but wonderful. Big, though. I cannot get in bedroom. I measure and measure. If I get in bedroom, then I cannot get in after. Very big.'

'Where do you propose putting it?' I sneezed again. I felt as though there were only one kind of new clothes which I might need, and I would not care, and neither would I know, whether they were well sewn or not.

'I consider maybe' – Pisa was nervously anxious – 'maybe in hallway?'

'Won't there be a draught?' Now, I thought, I shall never be able to come in or go out without being greeted or sped on my way by Pisa, sitting in the hall, turning the handle of some beastly machine.

'Oh no, please, no. I can fetch electric fire from bedroom if entirely necessary.'

'All right,' I agreed, weakly. I wanted to tell her about leaving on the electric fire. I wanted to protest about the machine, but a great engulfing shudder overcame me, and I could do nothing but give in.

'You are not well?' Pisa sounded concerned. 'You have grippe?'

I said, yes, I thought I had, or soon would have. I liked the idea of having the grippe; it sounded less trivial than an ordinary cold in the head.

'You go to bed. I prepare hot grog.' She was competent, grateful.

I told her where my purse was, and asked her whether she would be kind enough to get me half a bottle of whisky.

She ran off, hatless, coatless, deaf to my admonitions, and I watched her feathering her way swiftly, lightly, through the snow.

I went into my bedroom, took off my shoes, and stretched myself out on the bed, covering myself with a rug. To get properly, and sensibly, into bed would be to allow myself to feel ill too easily. One must fight against it, and then collapse at the last. I don't know exactly why, but it is in our tradition.

When Pisa returned she handed me a glass of rich custardy eggnog; the consistency of zabaione. It was far from what I had wanted, but she stood over me while I ate it (it was too thick to drink) and made soothing noises of approval when I arrived, with some difficulty, at the last mouthful.

When she had gone I swallowed two aspirins, washing them down with a large glass of water which effaced the sticky remembrance of the eggnog. Then I went back under the rug and settled myself to sleep.

It must have been about an hour later when Pisa knocked softly at the door before entering. She smiled kindly at me, and whispered, conspiratorially: 'It is Bernhardt. He *insist*. You permit?'

'Oh no, Pisa. Must I? Just look at me. Can't you send him away? Or why don't *you* have a nice long talk with him instead?'

'Impossible. Am fetching machine. Anyhow it is you he want to see.'

'All right,' I said. 'Tell him I won't be long.' I felt cross, but flattered, too.

I crawled out of the rug, washed, made up my face again, and combed my hair in a different way, which looked merely strange, but strange enough to divert some attention from my rapidly pinkening nose and my heavy-lidded eyes.

I found Bernhardt waiting in the hall. He loped towards me, and kissed my hands. He was wearing an ancient top coat, greenish with age and neglect, which had evidently been very expensive in its day. The collar was of some rubbed and gingery fur, on which was a faint powder of dandruff. Around and about him was a slight odour of mildew.

'Ah, the poor Marianne,' cried Bernhardt. 'You are ill?'

I said yes, I was. I thought I might be getting influenza.

'Poor Marianne wishes to escape from life,' he said, putting his head on one side and regarding me thoughtfully.

'You can put it like that, if it pleases you. I just wish I were dead. And perhaps I shall be soon.'

'The real deep death wish. Very interesting.'

'You make a note of that in your survey,' I said. 'And much good may it do you. It's my body, not my mind. Or doesn't that register?'

'Poor Marianne, you are angry because you are unhappy, and because you are unhappy you feel ill. We will talk all about it.'

Suddenly, unexpectedly, he produced a tiny thermometer from his pocket, slipped it out of its case, and popped it into my mouth.

We stood there, staring at each other.

He removed the thermometer and looked at it carefully. 'You have temperature much below, which is the prelude to a fever. That proves you are sad; your spirits not good. We shall see what we can do.'

'Yes,' I agreed, but without much hope. 'You see what you can do.'

'If Marianne will tell me what is the matter,' he coaxed as though I were a child.

'It's only that I don't feel well. And you needn't push that bit of glass in my mouth and then tell me that my spirits are low, because I know better. And I've nearly finished typing a novel which has depressed me utterly – it's so long, and so silly. Then there's Pisa who is going to bring a machine belonging to Mrs Vassenheimer and put it in the hall, and alter all her clothes, and remake me entirely if I don't look out –'

'So Pisa is behaving naughty and worrysome?'

'No, she isn't,' I contradicted.

Bernhardt sighed. 'You must continue,' he said, 'and then we will make a study of your tensions.'

'I don't see what good a study of my tensions, as you call them, is going to do.'

'First there is the novel, then Pisa, and what else has upset Marianne?' Bernhardt was patient, but persistent.

'And Alexandra has a new boy friend –' I began.

'Ah, there is your fever, the first cause,' Bernhardt interrupted triumphantly. 'Alexandra has found herself a new boy friend, as you put it, and you have none, and so you wish to die, thinking yourself neglected and unloved. Very interesting. When women suffer neglect they feel the death wish. It is well-known, but seldom does one have such absolute proof.'

'It's nothing like that. I don't want him. He isn't my type. I don't even like him. Alexandra doesn't like him all that much, either.'

'*She* does not like him?' Bernhardt pondered on this for a few seconds. It was apparently beyond his scope. 'Then what are your deductions? Has he any hold upon her?'

'Only one,' I said. 'The usual one. So many men turning out to be not quite what they seem, and this one obviously *is* what he seems. At least, in one particular.'

'What you say is that Alexandra,' he hesitated, 'lacks the final consummation which would make her aware of herself as a woman?' It was evident that he had chosen his words carefully, for reasons of delicacy, and also out of regard for the lowest possible mean of my intelligence.

'I wouldn't happen to put it like that. What I would say is that she may need the security of an acceptable relationship, which, apparently, is becoming rarer nowadays. And that doesn't apply only to Alexandra.'

'You feel it, too?' he asked, with bright interest.

Sometimes, I said, but not often, nor so urgently, being older, and perhaps more choosy. 'Besides, I have my ways and means.'

Yes, he said, morosely, he supposed I had.

I liked Bernhardt very much; I felt his friendliness cosily tucking me in; but somehow it could go no further.

Bernhardt stared at me and breathed gustily. 'Do you think

I could change my life altogether, upside down?' he asked suddenly.

'I don't know. But my guess is that you couldn't.'

'If I tell you my life in detail, then perhaps you consider and think otherwise?'

'I've had all this kind of thing before,' I protested weakly. 'And it hasn't turned out a bit well. Not for anybody. And I can't cope with facts just now. I can't cope with mental surveys without facts, either. I just feel very, very low.'

'Most interesting,' he said, as though he were thoroughly bored. Then he shook himself into crossness again. 'Why did you last time say do this, do that, go to Jog and Bottle, bring this, bring that, and so, if you do not want to know about me and are not serious with me?' He began to get agitated and mislaid his English.

'I'm very fond of you. I like you. That's serious enough, isn't it?'

'No. You will excuse me if I say that you are a woman about whom we read much – the English virgin.'

It is always difficult to keep one's sense of humour, and nearly impossible to keep it when one has a cold. 'I am certainly not a virgin.' I felt, and sounded, most affronted.

'And therefore you are wicked, being not what you appear.'

At that moment, thank goodness, I heard Pisa return. Her excited voice trilled out confused instructions to what sounded like an army behind her. There was a banging about and much shuffling of feet. Then a man's voice swore, comprehensively.

I looked at Bernhardt.

'I will go and see.' He sounded subdued.

He returned almost immediately. 'It is Pisa,' he announced, unnecessarily. 'She has two rough men bringing in an organ.'

'Bringing in a *what*?' Then I pulled myself together. 'It isn't an organ. It must be Mrs Vassenheimer's sewing machine.'

'Perhaps.' Bernhardt nodded disinterestedly. 'It is very large. I am sorry if I behave badly, but I have caught an infection of the liver.'

I said I was sorry, too, about everything, and especially about his infection of the liver.

Then he said that he, too, was broke, otherwise he would take me out to dinner.

I tried to comfort him by suggesting that after Pisa had got the machine settled in, and there was peace and quiet again, I would make us both a Welsh rarebit.

'Very nice,' he said. 'You are a good woman.'

I felt utterly defeated. There is something about being a good woman which instantaneously gets one down.

'And why are *you* broke?' I asked, almost accusingly. It is bad enough to be broke oneself, but if all one's friends are the same, then it is even worse. One can hardly allow oneself the small relief of complaining, without bringing a counterblast of louder complaints about one's ears.

'Many reasons. One, I do not add up right, and I think the bank do not add up right. But they do.'

'Well, I thought you'd be able to add up. That's your kind of thing, isn't it?'

'Only in big ways. I deal with results, not with the small steps. Then there is the question of income tax. It is difficult for us to remember that in this country you pay.'

'Yes,' I said. 'It is a snag, isn't it?'

Then he said that he had a few shillings, and would, with my permission, go and get us some beer to drink with the Welsh rarebit. I don't really like beer, but I thought that with money as it was – or wasn't – I had better try to acquire a taste for it.

While Bernhardt had gone for the beer I decided to inspect Mrs Vassenheimer's machine. It wasn't as big as an organ – not quite. But it was formidable. Pisa was standing by its side, obviously entranced. She said it was the loveliest thing she had ever seen, and she could save me lots of money, and make lots of money for herself with it.

I asked her who on earth she had found to cart it in at that time of night, and she told me that she had persuaded two men, who were sitting doing nothing by some red lamps and a hole in the road, to push it out of Mrs Vassenheimer's and trundle it along.

'It does not make a great noise, not as large as its size,' Pisa said placatingly.

I said I hoped not.

She sat down at the monster to show me that it did not make a great noise; within a few seconds she had impaled her finger on the needle and she screamed. I painted some iodine on her finger, which was all that the medicine cupboard contained, and bound it up.

Pisa said she thought she had better get acquainted with it in daylight, with which I fervently agreed. She refused my half-hearted offer of beer, when, and if, Bernhardt returned with any, and danced into her own room, humming happily.

'I am sorry,' said Bernhardt, 'if I keep you waiting, but I open my mind to the cold refreshment of the night air.'

I asked him whether he had thought up any way of making money quick, and he said he was concentrating on fundamental issues.

We made the Welsh rarebit together. I melted the cheese and Bernhardt poured a lot of beer into the saucepan, and then I had to put in some more cheese to soak up the beer. I cut the bread and Bernhardt let the toast burn; then I scraped off the worst of the burned surface because there wasn't any more bread. As a concerted effort it was masterly; we could hardly have produced a less appetizing meal. We ate in the kitchen.

'Do not trouble yourself,' Bernhardt said, kindly, retrieving a charred corner of toast from beneath the cooker. 'We are both sad, and bad food will suit us. It is a waste to send good food into an upset stomach.'

He might have put it more tactfully. We chased the chipped pieces of toast around our plates in silence, and drank the comparatively small amount of beer which Bernhardt had refrained from pouring into the saucepan.

'Have you got a tabulator on your writing machine?' Bernhardt belched.

When I said that I had he offered me the job of typing some reports for his department. I thanked him warmly and said that I needed any work I could get.

'You excuse?' From his pocket he fished out a small gold toothpick.

'I'm not all that keen,' I said.

'Is more hygienic than particles in the teeth.'

I told him that he must have been reading advertisements.

'That is better.' He sighed contentedly, but kept the toothpick at the ready.

'You ought to get married,' he said. 'It would suit you.'

There did not seem to be any adequate reply, so I just grunted.

'If you wish to be married, you would suit me very well. But you would not be suited *by* me?'

That took me back a bit.

'No, Bernhardt. I'm awfully sorry. Because I *do* like you.'

He began stabbing viciously at his teeth, digging out strands of cheese. He made a thorough job of it, which took quite a time. At last he was more or less satisfied, except for one morsel which continued to elude him.

'Please, Bernhardt, do stop that.'

'Do stop, don't stop, bring this, bring that, come here, go away, don't come back,' he hissed angrily through his teeth. Then he put the toothpick back in his pocket. 'And why do I not suit you?' He sounded belligerent. Perhaps the beer affected him.

That flummoxed me. I could hardly say 'Because of that horrible toothpick', and, besides, that wasn't all.

'For one thing,' I said, soothingly, 'if you're broke, you'd be broker if you married me, wouldn't you?'

That flummoxed *him*.

'You continue with your typing,' he said, after he had thought that one out. 'I am in a position to put work to you, plenty of work.'

'But I wouldn't want to. What's the use of my getting married if I had to continue with my typing? I might just as well stay as I am.' That could have been more happily phrased, too.

'So,' said Bernhardt, 'we could not do it. We will say no more.' He bowed slightly. I realized that his offer had been formally withdrawn. I bowed, too. It was a difficult moment. But Bernhardt said that he still had a few shillings and would, with my permission, get some more beer.

The beer hardly solved our problems, but it made them seem blurred and fairly far off.

'What is the name of Alexandra's new young man?' he asked suddenly. And when I said that it was Frederick, Bernhardt said that he remembered seeing some portraits of Frederick in Alexandra's flat.

'Unaesthetic.' Bernhardt had evidently been brooding on this. 'You should use your influence. It is not just to permit one's friends to do bad art.'

'I haven't seen any portraits of Frederick, aesthetic or otherwise. Anyway, I don't propose to use my influence. It's dangerous, and leads to disaster.'

'But you would not stand by and encourage inferior work?' Bernhardt was forbidding.

'I wouldn't encourage it, but I would stand by.'

'That is the trouble today. People have no integrity. We do not *deserve* the world.'

'We haven't even got the world, have we?' I asked, sharply. Beer doesn't agree with me, either.

Bernhardt's face, always somewhat rubbery in texture, managed to contort itself to express contempt and resignation in large quantities. The contempt was uppermost.

'You have no soul,' he said abruptly. 'If you had a soul you would not wound me as you wound me. I ask you to marry me, and you say No. You do not do right in that. It is not kind. You should make a pretence to consider the proposal, and we arrange it most dignified, and afterwards, if you so wish it, you say No.'

'I'm sorry, Bernhardt. It was a great surprise to me. I did not expect it. I'm not used to being proposed to. Practically nobody has, ever. Except someone who was so impossible that he knew he was safe.'

'I comprehend that it is a new experience for you as I make the suggestion. If you had the habit of being more pleasant and more feminine, you would be proposed to, often.'

'Thank you, Bernhardt,' I said, humbly.

'That is why you feel so much of sentiment for young people who are able to present to you the knowledge of the existence of sexual desire without the involvement of which you have fear. It is why you do not take objection to unaesthetic portraits of Frederick, because he is a man, and young, and good-looking. Women are the same in all countries.'

'Please, Bernhardt, I'm so tired of talking about myself, and especially tired of talking about Frederick. I'm very fond of Alexandra, and that's the only reason I tolerate Frederick at all.'

'So?' He stared long at me. 'So that is the way it goes? The impetus of your affections runs to Alexandra?'

'Oh no, Bernhardt! You've got it all wrong.' I was exasperated beyond anger, almost beyond caring.

'Do not be fearful of me, little Marianne,' he said, kindly, pressing my hand. 'I understand very well. I am a fool to request you to marry me, feeling as you do for Alexandra.' He was apparently so much comforted that it would have been cruel to insist on disabusing him.

He kissed both my hands, and then, deferentially, pecked at my cheek.

We parted on a muted note of shared distress and irritation.

I wondered how that would fit into his survey, and I hoped that he would enjoy writing it all up.

When next I saw Alexandra she asked me whether anything exciting had happened, and I told her about Mrs Vassenheimer's machine, and how Pisa was providing unforeseen complications.

She said that somehow people always did.

'I had Bernhardt here a few evenings ago,' I said. 'Just when I was beginning to get the cold which I'm beginning to get over. He was complaining because I wasn't serious with him, or serious about him. The whole thing's a bit confused in my mind now. He actually asked me to marry him.'

'I knew he'd fall for you,' said Alexandra. 'And he is a frightfully nice man.'

'Yes, I know he is, but he looks so perfectly awful.'

'You could pull him together, couldn't you?' Alexandra asked.

'Even if I could, I don't fancy devoting the rest of my life to pulling anyone together. I'd rather be pulled together myself, for a change. And if that's too much to ask, then I can just about deal with myself, and no more. Supposing I did pull him together, I'd have to keep on doing it. As soon as one took one's eyes off him for two seconds he'd fall apart.'

'That's going a bit far. I'm sure you could train him – like a dog.'

'No, thank you. Any dog I've ever had has got out of hand in no time. Besides, pulled together or not, Bernhardt would still look awful.'

'Yes, I suppose he would. It's that kind of middle-class Mid-European middle age, isn't it? They always look as though they've been crumpled up and then wrapped round in fluffy blankets. It is a problem, isn't it? I'll try and rustle up someone else – someone who doesn't need quite so much spadework, if you see what I mean.'

I said that I did see, perfectly, but she mustn't try too hard.

The worst of my cold was over, but the aftermath was one pink and swollen eye, which ached and throbbed for no particular reason (the right eye), and two large spreading chilblains on one foot (the left). I felt justified in saying that I ached from head to foot.

I had had the doctor in that morning, who agreed that I was thoroughly run down and had prescribed a tonic: then he told me that *he* was even more run down, disgustingly overworked, and that his partner had just taken himself off to the South of France.

He then remarked that that was what we ought to do.

'Not together,' he added hastily, in case I got the wrong idea.

I said yes, I couldn't think of anything better, if it were not for the lack of money, and suchlike obstacles.

He said it wasn't only money with him, but the fact that he hadn't got a reliable partner, and he *had* got a wife. Both of which, apparently, made the obstacles larger and less easily surmounted, if they were not already insurmountable.

I found myself commiserating with him, and hoping that he would manage to survive; he said he hoped so, too, but he didn't sound optimistic.

I told Alexandra about this, and she groaned sympathetically. Then she asked me what I thought, all in all, about Frederick, whom, as far as I could gather, she saw every day. Obviously he hadn't cooked his goose.

'Just what I said before: I didn't much go for him.'

She said, no, she thought that, but Frederick grew on one.

Then she admitted that although Frederick did grow on one, and life was wonderful, really, she wished she could see her way out of the next few weeks.

'Work?' I asked. 'Not going well?'

'Hardly going at all. Even the cat book doesn't quite gel, and I'll have to ask for the advance in a day or two, although I'm not due for it yet. I've only one other thing on hand, a boy of eight, who's a fiend, but really. He chews caramels all the time so his face is always bulging this side or that, and he looks at me with the most grown-up contempt you can possibly imagine. I believe he knows I'm not much good, and he's intent on proving it.'

'You've probably got it all wrong,' I said, 'and he's admiring you no end.'

'I'm long past the stage of not recognizing a child's

expression, even if I can't get it. And if I could get his I'd probably be sued for it.'

She half-smoked three cigarettes, stubbing one out, then almost immediately lighting another.

'I've gone on to Weights,' she said. 'They keep me busier and I feel I'm getting more for the money.'

She sounded at screaming point, and I was tempted to tell her so, but a remaining vestige of good sense stopped me.

'What's that awful whirring noise that's just begun?' she asked.

'Pisa's machine. She's making Mrs Vassenheimer a yellow silk dress, and I can't thwart her because she hasn't paid last week's rent yet. She was very apologetic, and all that, but it didn't help much. She does lots of things in the flat which needn't be done, to make up for it, but that doesn't help much, either. So until she finishes the wretched dress neither of us will have any money.'

'Isn't it awful? There's always that. That's what everything comes to, in the end, or long before it, which is worse. I can't think what I can do. Even when I do work, I work so slowly, now, and I can't seem to get a run at it. And then I go out, to try to walk some ideas into my head and fingers, and when I come back I'm tired – so that's no solution, either.'

'You do sound in a bad way. But you have been popping off a lot lately, haven't you? You hardly give yourself a chance to get a run at it, as you say.'

'You know how it is. I get so restless, especially when things go wrong, and I begin to wonder what it is all about, this incessant worrying. There's only one life, and it would be nice to live it, for a change, wouldn't it?'

'Unfortunately there are the usual drawbacks: it's imperative to eat, and to pay the rent, and so on, and all this strolling about because it's a fine morning just gets one in a deeper mess. I know so well – I've done it. And it's damned difficult to stop doing.'

'Frederick's always saying something will turn up. Even his quarterly allowance hasn't turned up yet, although it's nearly two months overdue.'

'That can't be very jolly,' I said, 'Personally I'm a trifle bored with these turner-uppers. I've had some of them throughout the years, and many more years than you in which to suffer from the consequences. So often nothing does turn up, and yet they go on saying that it is sure to, and with such hopeful faces and such bright expectant eyes that it seems a pity to have to damp them down all the time. And they're so resentful of common sense. As the weeks go by and nothing happens, it always becomes the other person's fault for not having enough faith. They seem to rely a lot on faith – especially someone else's.'

'Yes, I've had some of that already, too. And my faith's wearing a bit thin. As against that there's the other and much more important side: we do seem to get on so frightfully well, in a quiet and solid way. He's so utterly different, and much more mature than Peter, for instance.'

'Peter's got your sort of background, though. I think if you could bring him to the point he's the better bet. If you must choose between the two.'

'I'm tired of struggling on by myself, and no one else has swum into my ken, and probably won't. And I'm sure Frederick's got a smell of genius about him. He only needs encouraging and pushing in the right direction.'

'Why not try encouraging him and see if anything happens? He's not doing much work at the moment, is he?'

'Actually, no, but then we do adore just being together,

which makes working a bit grim. The only thing I don't go for so much are all those evenings at the pictures. I sit there glazed and trance-like, and I come out feeling awful. I can't bear sitting and staring for too long.'

'Can't you explain that to Frederick?'

'Yes, I could, but he does enjoy it so, and that's terribly rare, isn't it?'

'Terribly rare,' I said, 'and terribly likeable, and it brings out all one's motherly instincts, and it's quite the simplest, sweetest bait.'

'I think you're a bit harsh, darling. I know it's for my good, and all that, but you don't seem to take any emotional reactions into account.'

I said I was sorry, and I thought it might be the mountain book, which was making me feel old and breathless, as if I'd climbed all the beastly peaks myself. And it made me feel older than ever to realize that I couldn't. Although it was a godsend at the moment, and I didn't know where I'd be without it.

Alexandra promised she would look out for any other dotty people who wanted manuscripts typed, and lure them in my direction.

'I do wish you got on better with Frederick,' she said. It would be such a comfort to me. One does need some morsel of approval now and then.'

'I don't feel I know the least bit about him.'

'He's awfully withdrawn. But that's one of the nice things. He's so equable and balanced, too.'

I said I was sure he was, and I couldn't see why he should be otherwise. He was having a pleasant time of it, and there was nothing to unbalance him, was there?

'People who aren't balanced get unbalanced without any reason. It's just their natures.'

'By the way, is Frederick ever going back to Australia? I mean if you cherish any dream of marrying him, would you actually go as far as that?'

'As far as which?'

'Both,' I said firmly. 'Marrying, and Australia.'

'As a matter of fact he does want me to marry him, and at first I was fairly certain I didn't want to, but as he keeps on and on it becomes much more attractive. It's so flattering being asked again and again. It puffs me up, and I must say I need it, everything else being so lowering. When I feel down like this I long to go and buy myself lots of clothes, and of course I can't because it all comes back to the question of money.'

'It's worse for me,' I said, 'I feel I'd like to be completely unpicked and reknitted in the shape I used to be. Massage, and face treatments, and fabulously expensive corsets, especially the corsets. They'd buck me up no end.'

'Oh, I don't know, darling.' Alexandra tried to console me. 'There's nothing quite so ageing as wearing marvellously fitting corsets. It shows one has so much to hide, doesn't it?'

I considered this, and it wasn't as consoling as it was meant to be.

'Well, it *is* worse for me, anyway.' I felt mulish. 'Even if I had the money for new clothes – which I haven't – that wouldn't do a thing for me, unless I could make myself look different to begin with, before I put them on.'

Alexandra studied me critically and dispassionately. 'You haven't really gone to pieces as much as many women do, at your age,' she said, kindly. 'I believe if you could begin to like yourself again, you'd look quite something.'

'Well, I can't. And I haven't now for a long time, and I wouldn't know where to begin.'

'Oh, darling, isn't it ghastly?' Alexandra flung herself at me in a puppyish way, and I realized the charm she must have, particularly for someone as balanced as Frederick, who probably hadn't ever been unbalanced by anyone before. 'But you look much better than you might do, considering, and we all have to go through the in-between stage, and we'll survive, God willing, to become grand old women, and be no end pleased with ourselves.'

I said I hoped so, but somehow I wasn't enthusiastic.

There are some people, and Frederick certainly was one of them, who seem to take one's small piece of a world by the heels, and turn it upside down, and shake it, so that nothing is quite the same again.

I became almost neurotically aware of his presence; his entrances and his exits were always, even if not consciously, recorded in my mind. I kept on thinking to myself, there he is again, going out with Alexandra; and there he is again, coming back with her. I began to listen for his footsteps, as though he were the only person who mattered to me, not merely that he mattered second hand.

I was quite pleased to find Peter hovering outside my flat one evening, because at least he wasn't Frederick. Peter asked whether he could come in for a few minutes.

He accepted a cigarette, and said he practically never smoked, but he thought he would, just this once. He didn't seem to get on with it very well.

'As a matter of fact I didn't actually come to see you, but Alexandra's out,' he explained with customary lack of tact. Tact is not fashionable nowadays. Or perhaps it is a quality which men seldom need to acquire. They get on excellently without it.

'Did you expect her to be in?' I asked.

'She used to be,' he said.

'She quite often isn't now.'

'I've tried her on the telephone, too, but there's never any reply.'

'She might not answer if she were working,' I suggested.

Peter considered this, then shook his head, and said he thought she would, at least she used to.

'Is there anything the matter, do you think?' He studied me closely.

'Between whom?' I asked.

'Between me and Alexandra,' he said, doggedly. 'We used to see a lot of each other, and there was a special thing between us, if you get my meaning.'

'Perhaps you just took it for granted there was a special thing between you,' I suggested crossly. 'Perhaps if you'd taken the trouble to see that there was, it might have served your purpose better – if you have a purpose.'

By that time Peter looked cross, too.

'I might have known you'd turn out to be one of those women who say things which can't be pinned down.'

'I'm not proposing to be pinned down, not if I can help it.'

'I do think you might be a bit more cooperative. You might at least put a word in for me and see where I stand with Alexandra. Not that there was anything settled, but we did have, as I told you, a special kind of thing between us.'

Evidently he was by nature incapable of being explicit, or perhaps he, too, did not intend to be pinned down.

'Perhaps you didn't make it clear to Alexandra that you had this special kind of thing between you,' I said, patiently.

'I didn't have to. She knew. She often said we had. And we used to have our own sort of language, too. It was something

I've never had with anyone else, and neither has she. She told me so.'

The special language sounded quite horrid, and I suppose I must have shown my distaste because Peter said:

'You wouldn't know what I mean. But Alexandra's different. She's so young. And we used to laugh together and talk for hours, just as if we'd known each other all our lives.'

'Laughing together is all very well, but perhaps if you'd been a bit more positive, a trifle more grown-up yourself, this mightn't have happened.' Being continually relegated to the ranks of the middle-aged does not sweeten one's temper.

'That's just it,' said Peter. 'What has happened? I know there's some awful type named Frederick who hangs around all the time. But no one tells me anything. I asked Marius, but he said I had better ask you.'

I thought it was just like Marius to slither off, refusing to commit himself in any circumstances, and keeping on everyone's side.

I told Peter what I knew about Frederick, making my phrases as carefully vague as possible.

'An intellectual type.' Peter sounded depressed.

'He hasn't shown much sign of intellect in my presence, but I've only met him a couple of times.'

'You're not exactly smitten with him, are you?' Peter suddenly perked up.

I admitted that I wasn't.

'From the way you've described him he sounds the absolutely authentic hero, just what all the magazines are looking for,' Peter sneered.

'No, he isn't a bit like that.'

'What's the matter with him? Why don't you like him?' Peter persisted.

'I haven't the faintest idea. For instance I don't know why I *do* like you. You haven't ever behaved to me in any way which is likeable, and yet I feel that fundamentally you are.'

Peter brooded over this for a few seconds, then decided to take the better part of it and put the rest aside for future discussion.

'What do you suggest I do, then?' he asked.

'What can you do, except to make up your mind? That is if it isn't too late.'

'Yes, but what shall I do in the meantime?' Obviously making up his mind could not be done on the spur of the moment, and a pretty long interval must elapse.

'You could at least ask Alexandra out properly, instead of just calling her up whenever the mood takes you,' I suggested.

'I tried something like that once, only it didn't turn out brilliantly. Didn't she tell you?'

'Vaguely,' I prevaricated.

'You wouldn't think so much could go wrong in such a short time,' he said. 'And Alexandra behaved most oddly. I simply don't know what came over her.'

'Perhaps nothing did,' I said. It was cheap but irresistible.

He gave me a sidelong chilly stare.

'I don't think you've got the hang of it at all,' he said. 'You've heard Alexandra's point of view, and I expect she made me look all sorts of a fool. But she was so inconsistent. First she seemed to edge away as though I was going to set upon her, and on the way back when I felt like death she spent hours staring out of the window and not saying a word. And in the middle she was frightfully coy and come-hither, and I've always liked her so much because she wasn't either.'

'Perhaps you thought she was being coy when it was just

nervousness. And maybe you felt guilty because you knew she might want more than you wanted.'

Peter gave me another cold stare. We were obviously getting too near the knuckle.

'I can't understand her mulling it all over with you, either. That isn't like her, or wasn't.'

'Well, you're mulling it over with me, to some extent, aren't you?'

'Yes, but only because you've made it fairly plain that you're in the know, but only half in the know, because you've only heard her side of the story.'

'I don't want to hear any more sides of any stories. But I do advise you, if you have any real feelings for Alexandra, to make some positive move. Can't you hoick Frederick out of the way?'

'Quite frankly, Marianne, you do surprise me.' Peter's voice became more remote and overbred. 'I thought you were just a bit above that kind of talk. That's all women seem to think about, the old mossy idea of competition, and pitting one man against another. It's frightfully dated, you know. One simply doesn't feel like that.'

'If you don't, then what are you fussing about?'

Peter scowled and said he would write to Alexandra, and see whether she were better at answering letters than at answering the telephone.

He expected everything to be very very easy, which it seldom, if ever, is.

Pisa said that Mrs Vassenheimer was delighted with the yellow silk dress. And because Mrs Vassenheimer was delighted, Pisa was able to pay me last week's rent and part of a week in advance.

'And why should she not be pleased with it?' Pisa asked, as though I were arguing with her. 'It made her look svelte as svelte, big as she is in the bust, and with a lump round her middle which it is difficult to conceal.'

I said I was sure it was, and could Pisa conceal mine?

She looked me over critically, and then asked me to turn this way and that, as though she had never seen me before, but perhaps the professional approach was entirely different.

'Yes, you are difficult, too,' she said. 'Because as well as a lump you lack shoulders. But that we can come over.'

It did not sound too promising, but I felt a sudden surge of joy at having been paid, however small the amount. It was a good omen for the future. It was arranged that Pisa should see what she could do about my clothes, and in return she would not pay me next week's rent, so that she could give me her whole attention.

Pisa beamed and thanked me, and I thanked her, and we both began to believe that life was wonderful, and everything still to come – although for Pisa everything was still to come. Her gaiety took over the flat, and for a while infected even me.

I smiled at myself in the mirror as I passed, and I noticed what an improvement that was.

'You wear all the wrong colours,' Pisa said. 'So much black. It is like being at home again, in my own country, with always someone in mourning.'

I looked at Pisa, and I thought she might be right. It was one of her autumn crocus mornings; her hair coiled up, peasant-wise; her dress flame-coloured wool, tightly belted into her small waist; the sleeves pushed up, showing her smooth, biscuit-coloured arms; her elbows were youthful, softly rounded, with none of the drying, slightly wrinkled skin which mine had recently acquired.

She bustled about, glowing with good health, ripping my clothes to pieces, then taking them off to her machine to put them together again, occasionally chiding me for my carelessness.

'How come you allow it to fall?' she asked reproachfully, holding up a coat of mine, and putting her finger accusingly where the button ought to have been.

I said I didn't know how I'd come to allow it.

'You have spare perhaps?' she asked, eagerly. 'Is well made this coat. Hand-finished. You were given spare for sure.'

Realizing that I would do little about it, Pisa asked whether I would permit her to search, and she began to rummage through my work basket and my drawers, clucking sadly at the muddle she encountered. She spent hours winding up half-unravelled skeins of silks, and putting them into little compartments; she stitched away at my underclothes, sewing on shoulder straps and mending tears. Then she put everything away tidily. She found the button, which discovery filled her with disproportionate joy.

She made me stand up straight and hold my stomach in, while she pinned and tacked my clothes into slightly *outré* shapes.

'Please, Pisa,' I begged her. 'Not too tight. I can't sit down in this skirt, not with any safety. I simply must be comfortable.'

'A skirt is not for comfort.' Pisa was shocked. 'It is to be smart in. Slick over the hips, so. You come in after walking, and you do not sit in skirt. You put on house frock, very soft and full, and you sit in that.'

'If I remember,' I said.

'You remember because you cannot sit in skirt.'

Apparently she had the whole thing worked out.

When I was all pinned up and unable to move, the telephone

rang. Pisa answered it. When she returned to release me she said that the telephone call was for her, anyway, and she hoped I did not mind. It was Frederick, explaining how he had met Alexandra, and apologizing for not having got in touch with Pisa before.

'Is false this apology,' she said, biting off a piece of thread. 'He give it to me so that I give it to you, to get your favour because you are friend of Alexandra's, and Alexandra listen to you, which give you power on Frederick.'

The explanation was neat if not grammatical.

'Is scoundrel, this Frederick,' Pisa added calmly.

'What do you mean by that?'

'Is scoundrel type. Just is. Nothing to say more. People who are scoundrel not worthy of saying about. If I meet such scoundrel, I say to them, "Hello, darling, you do this nasty thing, and I push your face in it, and then you go home".'

I said that seemed a clean and simple way of dealing with the situation, and I liked the 'Hello, darling' greeting.

'A girl not English has to be smarter than English girl,' Pisa said, kindly. 'You have no need to push faces in the dirt. We have need.' Her pronounced accent and the arrangement of words showed me that this was a subject on which she felt deeply.

Pisa removed a few pins from her mouth.

'To be scoundrel type does not mean to be scoundrel. Only could be, if essential. Perhaps not essential, never,' she added, comfortingly. 'Now I give you example. I go out with Donald this evening who often bore me, but is not scoundrel, never.'

'How well do you know Frederick?' I was determined to get her back to the subject.

'How well?' She pretended not to understand. 'You mean how long?'

'No, I don't. I mean how well.'

'He is a young man who is easy to know well. Easy to know soon. Is no matter. I was not expecting more. Englishmen like to talk to foreign girls.'

I reminded her that Frederick wasn't English anyway.

She shrugged her shoulders. 'Australia – it is the same. Besides, it is me not English, not him.'

'It is I –' I began, and then gave up. The whole thing was too involved. And why should I care? I was getting lazier.

She told me that Frederick had spun her some story after the party where they first met, about being locked out, and having nowhere to go.

'I explain,' said Pisa, 'that he cannot come in because I have no home but stay as companion. And I think to myself, Poo, if that is all you want you are not the first. He ask me for address and I give him this one as it is just before I come here. Next time he arrive with Alexandra. That is all. It is nothing. It happen every day.'

I said yes, I was sure it did, after some parties. At most parties there is a Frederick, or a potential Frederick, especially if there is a Pisa around. And were I Frederick, and were I young, I might have tried it on myself, remembering that Pisa was a metal most attractive, and she appeared to be what she evidently was not.

Still in character as an Austrian peasant, Pisa gave a little bobbing half-curtsey and went back to her machine.

My first reaction was, what a succulent story I could tell to Alexandra. I might even be able to put her off Frederick for ever. Then I decided, for the good of my soul, to force my better nature uppermost. Perhaps being in love was what mattered, not whom one was in love with: that was of the least significance. As long as one still had the capacity.

I wondered whether *I* still had the capacity, lacking only the *bonne chance*. Which led me to think of Bernhardt, and wonder whether, had he been younger, and had I been younger, and if I could have dispossessed him of his toothpick, would I have married him? I came to the conclusion that I would not.

Even as a means of escape from the misery of a semi-basement flat, and the dank, forbidding horror of the laurel hedge which completely overshadowed the stale dirt-black mould in which nothing would willingly grow, which was supposed to be a garden, Bernhardt would not do.

Then I tried to imagine him in the country, and I pondered on what he would make of it, and what the country would make of him, and I decided that it would be a dead loss on both sides.

All of which led me to realize that Frederick was better than nothing and nobody, and perhaps Alexandra was right, after all.

So when next I saw Alexandra I was particularly kind, and tried to make amends for the mischief which I might have done, but had decided not to do. I even offered to lend her a couple of pounds, and she seemed grateful, but said that wouldn't be any good because she was past it.

'If I don't get the advance soon I'm *foutue*. I need about thirty to pay some bills, and the rest to live on until I get something else.'

'What about Frederick?' I asked tentatively.

She set her mouth stubbornly.

'You leave Frederick out of this,' she said. 'It's nothing to do with him, and I haven't got as low as that kind of sponging.'

I said I was sorry but I just meant had his quarterly advance arrived yet.

She said she hadn't the least idea, and, anyway, her

financial position was nothing to do with him, nor his with her. She sounded so affronted that I realized she must be much involved. Then she relented and became more herself again. She said that Peter had asked her out for a really special evening, and she didn't know what to do about it.

'What do you mean, you don't know what to do about it? You'd like to go out with Peter, wouldn't you?'

'Yes, but –'

'But what? You aren't exactly bespoken, are you? Not to the extent that you can't go out with anyone else, surely.'

'No-o . . .' She was doubtful. 'Except that that's not my kind of thing. If neither were important, then I'd be going out with dozens, if I could find them. But as they both are, in different ways – I mean as Peter definitely was and Frederick definitely is – I can't run them both at once, can I?'

I said I thought she was taking it all too seriously.

'Quite honestly, darling, it's time I took someone seriously, isn't it. Or, rather, that someone took me seriously. Frederick does, and Peter does on and off. But so much off that one doesn't know where one is. Now with Frederick I do know, and he says he knew from the first second, and he says you knew because you watched him.'

I admitted that I had watched him, and it was true that he could not take his eyes off her, and never had, within my sight, from that moment to this.

'I'm not awfully keen on the way you put it,' she said.

'Surely he doesn't want to monopolize every second of your time?'

'The thing is I do want to play fair, and it doesn't seem fair, with Frederick feeling as he obviously does about me, and me feeling as I think I do about Frederick, to go hopping off with Peter for the whole evening, does it?'

I lost my patience then, and said: 'Oh, for heaven's sake do as you please.'

At that Alexandra turned a bit sulky and said she would go and get some bread in the delicatessen across the road, and just pop in on the way back because there really was something quite factual which she wanted to ask my advice about. But she must go out first, otherwise the shop would be closed.

Just when she had gone Pisa came in, accompanied by Donald. She said they had been to hear a piano concerto, and afterwards they had talked to the pianist, who told them that it was impossible to live by music in England.

'In this so rich country you do not pay to hear music. You do not care. You turn the switch, and poo, no matter what come out, you listen.' I felt that they had rehearsed this on the way back. 'Is awful, no?' Pisa added, realizing that I was not sufficiently impressed.

I said I was sure it was awful, but I had no ear for music, except Schubert – and that only occasionally. Donald looked reproachfully at me.

'Schubert is dead. You support living music,' said Pisa, and Donald nodded his approval.

'We must make this a country where artists can live well. We must educate the people. But first we must educate ourselves.' Donald set his lips in a straight firm line to show that he was not going to stand any nonsense from anybody.

'Donald lend me Ruskin,' Pisa said proudly. 'I begin to read tomorrow.'

Donald smiled benevolently at her. She was obviously going to prove a perfect blend of pupil and follower. He must have had normal designs upon her, but they could come to the fore only after he had improved her mind. By which time Pisa would have got tired of him anyway.

'Which Ruskin?' I asked, trying to show an intelligent interest.

'Three books about stone in Venice,' said Pisa. 'They are good, yes?'

'Very difficult to read,' I said. 'I've never got through them. Only bits here and there. Wouldn't it be easier,' I asked Donald, 'to start Pisa off on something personal, such as *Praeterita*?'

'It is essential to approach the man through his work,' said Donald. 'The personal approach confuses the mind.'

'I still think it's more interesting my way round,' I protested weakly.

'You wouldn't read the life of a composer, or his letters, for instance, before listening to his work, would you?' Donald asked.

'I might,' I admitted.

Donald said, moodily, that that was the worst of women. They couldn't be objective. He managed to convey that I was a bad influence on Pisa.

The conversation petered out, and Pisa, after asking whether I minded, took Donald off to her room, where, supposedly, they were going to make a start on *The Stones of Venice*.

When Alexandra returned carrying a large loaf of black bread she said she was sorry if she hadn't seemed grateful for my advice about the Peter affair, but there was something else she really did want to tell me about, because she was in a bit of a spot.

At that moment we heard Pisa's soft and fluting laugh.

'Who's she got in there?' Alexandra asked, somewhat sourly.

'It's Donald,' I said.

'Oh, so she's got *him* now, has she?' Alexandra evinced a spark of interest. 'That boy does go the rounds, doesn't he?'

'He's improving Pisa's mind. They're starting on a course of Ruskin. The dreariest first, too.'

'Rather her than me. I can't say I envy that.' She was silent for a few minutes, clutching the bread which she refused to put down because she said she mustn't stay long as Frederick was waiting for her.

'Is he *always* waiting for you?'

'That's the point. He's got all his papers and so on upstairs. We thought we might as well work round one fire. It saves money.'

'As bad as that?' I was appalled.

'Well, sort of. And last evening he just dropped off to sleep, and what with the snow and everything I just hadn't got the heart to turn him out, so I covered him up with a rug and left him there. He was terribly stiff this morning. Of course that room's unspeakably draughty.'

'Didn't he wake up at all?'

'He didn't seem to. I mean, if he had he'd have said something, wouldn't he?'

'I suppose so. Unless he was pretending to be asleep for some purpose of his own.'

'Yes, but what purpose?'

'Why, so that he could stay, of course.'

'He didn't exactly get anything out of it,' she said. She glanced nervously at her watch, and said Frederick would be wondering what had happened to her.

'I hate all this checking up on people. It gives me the Iron Curtain creeps. Even if Frederick did go to sleep, why didn't you get rid of him this morning?'

'By that time he'd have been there already in the usual way, so there wouldn't have been any reason to turn him out then, would there?'

I said there was every reason, because by letting him stay she was creating a precedent.

'But then he looked so miserable I simply couldn't turn him out, especially after he'd hacked his face to pieces with my one and only razor blade, which is quite five years old. So that will teach him a lesson.'

'It will only teach him to bring his own razor next time.'

'He was terribly rueful and yet awfully sweet at breakfast,' Alexandra explained earnestly. 'He said he'd actually give up this grant and take a job so that we could get married. He said he'd learn to drive a tram – which was awfully touching and silly, don't you think?'

'Silly, certainly, especially as there aren't any trams nowadays.'

'Marianne, you're getting just about the end. You know perfectly well what he meant. It may not be practical, but it does show willing. I didn't think you'd be so unsympathetic.'

'I like you far too much to dole out lashings of spurious sympathy.'

'Yes, I know you do. I'm sorry. But sometimes everything piles up and I get frantic.'

'And now I'm going to give you my advice, whether you want it or not. Get rid of Frederick. Otherwise he'll move in and you'll never be able to shift him.'

Alexandra shuffled about a bit and said she couldn't bear to lose him.

'What was the idea of telling me about it, then?'

'I just sort of wanted you to know. It's such a comfort having you know what's going on, even if I don't take any notice of what you say. And supposing he does stay – and

I'm not saying he will – it's all quite proper in outlook. He'd marry me any minute. He actually suggested this morning that we should get a special licence.'

'That's a trifle rash, isn't it? Doesn't a special licence cost a lot?'

'There you go again! It isn't that I want him to spend his money on a special licence, and I wouldn't let him do it, but it's heaven to know he wants to.'

I said yes, I saw her point, and it must have been difficult to refuse.

'It would have been even more difficult if he hadn't looked a bit mucky and unkempt. If he'd been all spruced up I might have gone for it head over heels.'

Soon after Alexandra had gone, Donald, too, departed.

I asked Pisa whether she had had a good time with Ruskin.

'Poo,' she laughed prettily. 'That old man. He is damn bore, but no one read him. I take all those silly books, and next week I tell Donald I lo-ove to read Ruskin, and learn clever ideas, but it is a pity I know not enough English. So Donald work very hard to teach me good English, so I can speak better and read Ruskin. Is useful, no?'

'Very useful, except Donald's English isn't quite the best, and sometimes he forgets himself. You'll have to be careful there.'

Pisa looked quite agitated. She hated her small plans to go awry.

'He is not from good family?'

'I wouldn't say exactly that.' I was cagey. 'It's merely a question of intonation and inflection. What he says isn't wrong, but you might as well get the right tone while you're about it.'

'Oh, Marianne, I thank you. You are my friend. Because Donald speak quick and read much, I think he know everything, and I listen with much care. But you listen with ear and you hear wrong. Poo! I be very careful about Donald, you bet. And he give me dull books to read, and all close together – Ruskin and his stone!'

'You needn't be careful about Ruskin,' I said. 'It's only Donald.'

Even at the time I had a premonition that I ought not to have said that about Donald, and neither should I have said anything at all about Frederick.

I began to feel a net weaving itself about me, and I wished I could get away from them all, or, better still, that Alexandra and I could be back at the beginning again. Just the two of us, visiting each other occasionally, and talking and laughing together, before Frederick and Pisa or anyone else had come on the scene. I wished that Alexandra had kept her parties to herself, and left me typing away in my own flat, unheeded.

For a week or two all was quiet, if not exactly peaceful.

The snow had long since melted and a bleaker, blanker cold set in. The early afternoons began as swirling white mists and gradually thickened to yellow fog. The days passed quickly, as though the year was rushing towards its end; but the cold seemed to take on an air of eternity, as if there would never be warmth nor sun again.

My flat became appallingly chilly, and there were cross-currents of icy air which pricked around our ankles and stabbed at our shoulder blades.

Pisa took to swathing herself in a voluminous woolly shawl, which only she could have worn without appearing ridiculous, wide-striped as it was in cyclamen pink and black. This she wore over whatever else she happened to be wearing.

When she went out she draped it, cavalier fashion, pinning it on one shoulder with an enormous cameo brooch. She made a pleasure out of a necessity. Even so she was white-faced and not as exuberant as formerly. She crept out at different times of the day or evening, either to exercise Mrs Vassenheimer's animale, or to babysit, or to dog-sit, or to cook rich foreign foods for people who did not know how to cook and who wanted to give dinner parties. She made out moderately well; at least she paid her rent more or less regularly.

I ate quantities of the wrong kind of foods in a vain endeavour to keep myself warm, and all the clothes which Pisa had altered for me became tighter and tighter.

We were almost beyond talking; numbed into deathly silence. There was only one topic in which either of us had the least interest: whether or not the fuel for the boiler had arrived. And this was soon disposed of because more often than not it hadn't arrived. Apart from that we spoke only about the weather.

'Is damn cold,' Pisa would mutter, blowing on her fingers.

'Is dreadful,' I would agree, absent-mindedly. I had reached the stage where, instead of trying to correct Pisa's English, I spoke as she did.

Through the icy watches of the daytime I realized, or perhaps my mind registered without realization, that Frederick no longer went home, wherever home was for him. Evidently he had taken up residence at Alexandra's flat.

Perhaps it was the grey heavy cold, after the ephemeral sparkle of the snow, which put us all on edge.

Even Pisa remarked, balefully, that Frederick was always about and Mrs Aitch made several pointed observations, rudely phrased, on the amount of mud which some people brought in, trampling in and out and never wiping their large feet. She added, in case I had not understood, that she wasn't accustomed to having so many people using the top staircase and it all made more work, especially *some* people.

I began to wonder what the end of it all would be, and to wish more than ever before that I had kept myself entirely apart.

Only Alexandra, whom I saw usually from afar in those days, as she seldom visited me, had overcome the heaviness of the cold-laden air.

She was in that state of youthful amazement which we can so soon look back upon and laugh about, and which is so easy to mock; she really was, however disastrously, in love.

She walked surrounded and enclosed by her own pleasure. The kind of love which can live only in itself, breathe its own atmosphere, and which can hardly be spoken to.

Frederick, an unknown quality of need and desperation, walked always by her side.

With the surprised pang of the old, once familiar ways of loving being relived before my eyes, I watched Alexandra, a small, tense, aware figure, as she stepped out, her hand resting in Frederick's hand.

She looked slighter still, more fragile, and she walked lightly, as though she were ready, for the very joy of it, to take off, and to fly above the ordinary pavements, and the dank laurels, and the red-bricked, blind-faced houses.

And I remembered swiftly, and with some astonishment, what it used to be like; this uncomfortable ecstasy of being, perhaps for the first time, wholly in love, beyond the realization of any other existence except the present trance-like state. All ordinary life, all commonplace requirements of books and music, and the presence of friends, temporarily banished by this exclusive desire for the nearness of one other person – until the critical creature at the back of one's mind takes over, and one's everyday self comes back again.

Viewed from the outside, it is saddeningly absurd; frighteningly dangerous.

Although Alexandra looked happy enough when she was actually with Frederick, she looked merely worried and guilty when she was away from him.

On one of her rare visits to me she said that we would only have a few minutes together because Frederick was 'calling' for her. For once she refused a cigarette, because she was trying to do without them, being cheaper, and anyway Frederick did not really approve of women smoking.

'How's it working out? You and Pisa?' she asked casually.

'It goes towards the rent,' I said. 'And you were right. Pisa's not nearly as exotic as she makes herself out to be. Taken all in all, she's quite a homely type. And how's it working out, you and Frederick?' I asked.

'So you know he's more or less moved in? Well, it's cheaper, and easier, in lots of ways, except for work, and then I do find him a bit ever-present. Still, there's bound to be something not in favour. But I can't imagine what I'd do, or even what kind of person I'd be, or if I'd be a person at all, without Frederick. I can't even remember what it was like, before. Except I know it must have been dreadful.'

'You have got it badly, haven't you?' What with the cold, and the draughts, and the shortage of money, I wasn't in the mood for romantic outpourings. Sitting in the sun I might have supported them better.

'You simply don't understand. It happens, or it doesn't. Of course you're older and you weigh up, for and against. But this isn't like that. It's more a song that either gets you, or doesn't, the first time you hear it.'

She was so evidently enchanted that my disenchantment was a heavy burden.

'It's so odd, though. I'm wildly happy, but worried near to demented, and all at once, which makes me quite light-headed.'

'Money, I suppose?'

She nodded. 'We don't even eat out now. Not even round the corner with something called meat paste on soggy toast, for one and three a round. Then there's coffee at eightpence, real English coffee, half mud, half acorns, and I always wonder how they manage to make it taste so nasty so that I can avoid it. That comes to one and elevenpence each – no, one and elevenpence for me, and three and twopence for Frederick, because he always has a double portion of meat paste, although how he *could* ... And that makes six bob with tip, and not exactly nourishing or sustaining. So we've taken to onion soup upstairs, with lots of grated cheese, and sometimes we sprinkle revolting dried herbs in, too, which makes it taste different, if not better – and an orange apiece afterwards for vitamin C. It's all most cunningly worked out, although a trifle tedious. My stomach knows what's coming to it, and sends up little pleading messages saying, *Oh, please, not again!* But on the whole it's cheaper, much, and better for one than meat paste, don't you think?'

I said I was sure it was.

'But the relentlessness of it, darling, that's what gets me down. Still I expect we'll come through, and everything will be quite perfect once we get organized.'

I didn't like to remember how many years I'd been saying that to myself, and still I wasn't 'organized', nor likely to be, alas.

'And how does Frederick react to all this?'

'He keeps on saying how sorry he is, because he'd rather

give me the world, and so on. But he thinks it a great lark, too, and he's got plans, galore. He says he'll sell my drawings for the cat book, and get guineas apiece (if they're mine to sell, but we haven't gone into that yet) and we'll be rolling in money. Then we'll up and off on some cargo boat, half round the world, and lie in the sun and eat lichees, or whatever one does eat, and then we'll come back, brown as brown, and be ready to slave like mad, and make lots more money, and do it all over again. By the way, if anything did really happen, and we could go off, would you look after Tom for me? I know it's a lot to ask –'

'I thought Tom was only lent to you while you did the cat book?'

'So did I, but everyone seems to have forgotten about him, and I'd miss him now, although he's still practically the deadest cat living I've ever come across. He's not a nuisance, except for his box, and that's not as bad as it might be. And his food, but he's not particular. Actually he's been having onion soup with us, lately, things being as they are.'

'Does he have an orange, too?' I asked warily.

Alexandra looked quite perturbed. 'No, I hadn't thought of that. But he does have special cat tablets, two a day, at one and nine for sixty, to make up any deficiency. And he's thriving in coat, although his mind's as blank as ever.'

'All right,' I agreed, grudgingly. 'I'll have Tom. Not that I believe in the cargo-boat idea for one minute, and you needn't think I do.'

'I knew you'd have Tom if it ever came to it,' she smiled. 'And do try to believe in the cargo boat, because if we all believe frantically, then it might come true.'

Talking of money, she said Frederick had a scheme he wanted to put up to me, and he ought to be here by now.

I refrained from commenting on this. I did not like the sound of it.

The realization that Frederick would arrive soon seemed to throw her into a state of nervous excitement. Suddenly she asked me whether I had noticed any difference in her.

'You look much thinner,' I said, trying hard. Had I missed my cue? 'More ethereal.'

'Not more experienced? As though a lot had happened to me?'

'Perhaps.'

'I never knew,' she said, 'there was so much to know.'

I nodded, non-committally.

'Much more than you can possibly imagine,' she said. Perhaps she thought that I had spent my whole life typing other people's manuscripts.

'And all that one's read doesn't give one the least idea,' she said.

Maybe it was the general beastliness of the day, or perhaps the general beastliness of growing older, or the grim expectancy of Frederick who would be with us soon, but whatever it was I was hard put to it not to snub her, and to tell her that long, long ago I had read the many tedious volumes of *The Scented Garden* and, by reason of those, if not by direct experience, I was to some extent acquainted with the gist of what she was trying to say – but even one's private devil is occasionally merciful, and mine held me back.

'So much and so much is wonderful at first,' I said.

'But, darling, if you'd ever known *this*, you'd never forget it.' Alexandra was breathless with discovery.

'I could, you know. It's incredible what one can forget. And very, very comforting, too, although you wouldn't believe it.'

'Isn't it odd, when there was nothing, I could talk about it. Now there's so much I just can't say a word.'

'That doesn't apply to me. I've so little to tell that I can say it over and over again.'

'But you must have something else, apart from this' – vaguely she waved her hand to include the typewriter and the table strewn with a muddle of papers – 'and apart from me, and Frederick. You must have something else.'

'Perhaps,' I said, 'but that's another story.'

She began to tease me, affectionately, as she used to do, and then suddenly became silent as soon as Frederick arrived.

Frederick came in carrying a bottle of sherry-type wine, some of which we drank. The effect was not exhilarating.

Alexandra kittened around him in a way which was almost pitiful. It was apparent that she was becoming frightened of him, and wanted to keep him sweetened up against the time when they would be alone together. I felt sorry for her, and yet I remembered that once I had behaved like that, and although I had regretted it since, nothing and no one could have stopped me.

'Has Alexandra told you all our news?' he asked, absent-mindedly helping himself to a handful of salted almonds and cramming them into his mouth.

'I've heard about Tom and the cargo boat,' I said, refraining from mentioning the palmy days of meat paste which were gone, and the onion soup period which was now upon them.

'Hasn't she told you she's going gadding, as soon as my back's turned?' Frederick grabbed a curling strand of Alexandra's hair, and tweaked it playfully, but not too gently.

Alexandra launched upon a gabbled and nervous explanation of how Peter had asked her again and again to go out with him to dinner, but she had always said she couldn't, only now that Frederick had to go out himself with a man who was only over here for a short time, and who was something to do with the grant, she thought she might as well accept Peter's invitation, and as Peter happened to be free the next evening, and as it was the next evening when Frederick had to go out . . . and so on, explaining and excusing herself.

Meanwhile Frederick scowled; from the thickening atmosphere which had spread itself around him I realized that, when roused, he could have a very nasty temper indeed. No wonder Alexandra kittened about. She had good reason.

'I don't want to go myself, but mine's a command performance,' he said. 'And that's very different from choosing to go off.'

'Why? What's wrong in that?' I asked. 'I think it will do her good, don't you?'

'But, darling, if you'd really rather I didn't go –' Alexandra began, desperately anxious for Frederick's approval, or, at least, for the cessation of his obvious disapproval.

'Why should Frederick rather you didn't go?' I asked snappishly, forgetting my role of non-participator.

Frederick gave me a quick venomous glance. Then he turned to Alexandra and tweaked her hair again. 'But once we're married, I warn you, I shan't let you out of my sight.'

Alexandra nuzzled up to him, tremulously eager to be put in the stocks for ever and ever, if that was what Frederick really wanted.

We had some more of the sherry-type wine, but that didn't help much, and Frederick ate another handful of salted nuts.

'It'll be your last chance' – he smiled tigerishly at Alexandra, and winked at me, to show me that it was all a joke – 'because I'm going to be a real old-fashioned type of husband, and I shan't let you out of my sight.' He chuckled deprecatingly, inviting me to share in the fun.

'And are you sure that Alexandra wants to become such an old-fashioned type of wife?'

Alexandra held herself tensely, tight and timid, trying to make herself invisible so that our sparring could not touch her.

'It's a question of moral issues,' said Frederick. 'I just don't believe in husbands or wives gadding off without each other.'

'You're a nice one to talk of moral issues –' I began hotly.

'And if you're thinking of my position now, it's an invidious one, and *not* what I wanted, as Alexandra will tell you.' Frederick was firm and haughty and self-righteous.

'Oh yes, Marianne, dear, that's perfectly right.' Alexandra almost choked over the words, she was so anxious to stop our bickering going further. 'I persuaded Frederick to stay. I did, really. It seemed better, and easier, and everything, and as we're going to get married anyway, what does it matter?'

What I thought did matter, although I did not say so, was Frederick's monstrous behaviour.

'As I keep on telling Alexandra, we ought to get married *now*, and we would have been married before now if I'd had my way.' Frederick's anger was chilly, controlled.

'I know we ought to,' Alexandra began, hesitantly.

'What's the good of getting married just because you think you ought to?' I asked. 'What's the point? Until you're sure, that is. You don't want to live unhappily ever after, do you?'

Frederick was pale with rage, but he dared not loose it upon me. Unfortunately I knew that Alexandra would receive the full force of his caged-up bitterness when they were alone together, and I wished that I had held my tongue.

'You tell her, Alexandra, you tell her. This is farcical.' Frederick managed to sound like a patient soul in torment.

'It is my fault entirely,' Alexandra quavered. 'But, as I keep on saying, it's so awful to think of getting married literally without a penny. And in rags. Or what feel like rags. Clothes that I'm so sick of I can hardly look at. I know it's trivial, and all that, but those kinds of things do matter, even if they ought not to.'

I said I was sure they did matter, and Frederick said, sulkily, that that was what he really wanted to talk to me about: making money. Obviously that was why he had not let his temper rage before this. He did not want to acknowledge our enmity openly, in case I might be prevailed upon to be of use to him.

'I'm going to chuck up that damned grant,' he said, sitting back and looking very large and square and determined, 'and get myself into the kind of racket that'll keep us both, and buy Alexandra all the clothes she wants, until something better turns up.'

'What kind of racket?' I asked.

He smiled to himself. 'Selling,' he said. 'Just selling. You can sell people anything if you go about it in the right way. And that's something I do know about, never mind how. Buy up any line, cheap, lumberjackets, duffle coats, binoculars, cameras, any damn thing, and advertise, and you get the money rolling in. If they're bargains people will buy them, whether they want them or not.'

'Advertising costs money,' I said, although this was my least objection. I wondered what Alexandra thought about this, but decided not to ask her. She was sitting very still and unrelaxed.

'Not the kind of advertising I mean; cheap and vulgar, maybe, but it rings the bell. Might do it privately at first;

Roneo a few thousand letters and see what the response is. If I did go into that line could you run off a few thousand feelers, to test the market?'

I said that I was very sorry, but I just couldn't. I hadn't the time, and besides it wasn't my kind of thing. I left it vague, but I think he knew what I meant.

He said, surprisingly meekly, that he quite understood; he looked as though he understood only too well.

'If I were you,' I said, 'I'd forget about these wild money-making schemes, and get on with your book, or thesis, or whatever it is. Besides, you've accepted the grant, haven't you? Surely it wouldn't be strictly ethical to go back on it now?'

He muttered something about making a name for himself, and showing everybody, and that anyway they wouldn't starve.

'Marianne doesn't approve of our goings-on, but then she doesn't know what it's like to be in love, does she, pet?' Almost threateningly Frederick put his hand around Alexandra's waist and pulled her closer to him.

'Leave me alone. Marianne will be sick in a minute, won't you, darling?' Alexandra made a small protest, but I believe she knew that she would pay dearly for it.

'I might,' I admitted, 'especially as you've got all night to sit in each other's laps.'

Frederick did not say a word, but the pallor around his mouth was more pronounced; he looked as though he were ill-wishing me with a quiet concentration.

Alexandra, trying to retrieve the moment, asked me what I was doing, and I told her I'd finished the mountain book, and had just begun on three one-act plays for an amateur dramatic society. All capital letters and stage instructions underlined in red, and one ought to be paid double, but one wasn't.

Then I asked her what she was doing, and she said nothing new except one baby, pastel, and only five guineas, which was the lowest she had ever accepted. 'Of course, it's got practically no face,' she said, 'just a couple of pale-pink bulges, and no hair, either, so I don't suppose it's worth more, but still –'

'A bloody squally brat.' Frederick sounded vicious.

'No, it isn't,' Alexandra said sharply. 'I'm good with real babies, tiny babies, but you had to go over and talk to it, and make it cry. All that ridiculous tickle wickle under the chin – babies simply *hate* it. Besides, you only do it to show off.'

Frederick looked blacker than ever, then suddenly turned upon me and said I was a bad influence on Alexandra, and she never used to be like that, then for a few minutes we all shouted at once, then Frederick, somewhat surprisingly, apologized to me, and half apologized to Alexandra, and we all simmered down. It was a short but quite shattering interlude.

Then they took themselves off, and I was glad to see them go.

3

The Repercussions

I HOPED THE EVENING WAS OVER, BUT THAT WAS where I was wrong, because it was that evening that the repercussions really began. Although they began in a small way.

Donald arrived without warning. After asking for Pisa, and on being told that she was out cooking somebody's dinner, he asked whether he might come in. I said he could if he wanted to, but I managed to make my voice express my surprise that he should want to. Donald, however, was undeterred.

He had brought a half-pound box of chocolates, obviously intended for Pisa, which we ate as we sat huddled around the fire.

We talked for half an hour or so, in short sentences, about nothing at all.

At one point Donald brightened up and said that he had applied for a job as a clerk in the Town Hall, and did I think he might get it?

I said I didn't know, not knowing how good his clerking

was. Which was honest, but unwise. I would have done better to butter him along.

'Not good enough to be a bloody clerk in the Town Hall? So that's it, is it?' Suddenly he was much upset.

'Now, Donald, what on earth is all this about? There's no reason to speak like that. It's rude and quite uncalled for.'

'Now I'm finding out what the whole lot of you is like,' he muttered. 'I'm not good enough even to *speak* to you, nor to Pisa, neither.'

'What *are* you talking about?' A nasty clammy feeling flickered down my spine, and I could have shaken Pisa.

'You know what I'm talking about as well as I do,' he said.

'I don't.' I was playing for time, and thinking how vastly unfair it all was.

'And I know, and you know I know, that you told Pisa I wasn't good enough for her, nor good enough for her to talk to,' he said angrily.

'Oh, Donald, don't for heaven's sake start that nonsense; and besides, it wasn't like that, I swear it wasn't. It came about because of Ruskin, and what Pisa said, and then what I said, but it didn't mean what it seemed to mean on the face of it.'

'What *did* you mean?' Donald was relentless.

'Only that Pisa ought to learn English from someone qualified to teach her English. Why, I've begun to talk like Pisa, not Pisa like me,' I said wildly, but truthfully.

'That wasn't what Pisa said, and it wasn't what Pisa gave me to understand you meant.' Donald was tenacious.

'Maybe I wasn't exactly precise, but that *was* what I meant ...'

'Then why did you tell her not to bother to read Ruskin? Do you think Ruskin would hurt her? Isn't *he* good enough for you?' Donald had been much wounded, that was apparent.

'I didn't say anything of the kind. Pisa told me she couldn't read Ruskin, it was too difficult, and I said she ought to learn how to speak English before she could hope to understand Ruskin. No, I didn't. I'm sorry. Pisa said that. I'm getting confused myself.'

'I should say you *are* getting confused.' Donald's opinion of women, always fairly low, was sinking fast. 'Pisa said you told her not to listen to me because I don't speak proper.'

'There you are.' I was triumphant. 'Why, you're speaking just like Pisa yourself.'

'No I'm not,' he snarled. 'I'm speaking just like me.'

'Then you don't speak proper.' I was stung to the futile retort.

'You've had every advantage, and expensive schooling, I dare say, and you've not made much of it, from what I can see. And then you tell me I can't speak proper, and you put Pisa against me. A nice girl like that I enjoy taking out. It's not right, that it isn't, and I don't believe in interfering busybodies.'

There was some justice in what he said, although some injustice, too. And yet I had intended no harm, but, of course, I ought to have known better than to expect Pisa to keep quiet.

Silently, malevolently, we sat glaring at each other. Oddly enough we continued to eat chocolates, handing them backwards and forwards, politely, and pointing out to each other which was which, and deferring to each other and bowing over the last coffee cream which, in the end, Donald insisted that I should eat.

'I'm really sorry, Donald,' I said, 'but it wasn't at all what you think it was, and no offence meant, and all that. Whatever is said sounds different from what is intended.'

He said yes, he supposed it did, but he was far from happy, although slightly more resigned.

'I ought to have known,' he said, 'that I was a fish out of water, and that no good would come of it. But I did think at least that you were kind.'

That hurt me more than anything else, and I sat there, swallowing hard, feeling ashamed of myself.

Suddenly Donald said that after all he didn't want to see Pisa, because he didn't feel like seeing anybody, and with a few incoherent phrases, half smoothing over, he took his leave, and rushed off in a panic of anxiety to be gone.

When Pisa came in I was waiting for her.

'I've had a very nasty time with Donald,' I told her, 'and it's entirely your fault. And I feel sick because I've eaten far too many chocolates, and, indirectly, that's your fault, too. Why did you have to tell Donald that I told you not to listen to him because he doesn't speak properly? Why?'

Pisa's face puckered up. 'Is not fair! Damn fool Donald ought to shut up!'

'That isn't the point. *You* ought to have kept quiet. I only made a vague suggestion, for your good, and look what happens. It was perfectly awful. Besides, you've hurt Donald, and I've hurt Donald, and neither of us wanted to do that.'

Pisa sniffed sadly. 'Was Donald's fault,' she said. 'He took me to damn boring play reading. We sit in the cold for hours and hours, and everyone take it in turn to read except me. Each time the teacher behind the counter smile at me, and nod for me to read a piece, Donald say, very quick because he feel embarrassment for me: "Not her, she cannot speak English." And there I sit in the cold, and not permitted to read, and I feel worse and worse, and when we come out we go to dreadful place in middle of road, like tent, and drink nasty tea, and I say to Donald, "Not so much of my not speak English, and why not should I not read the same like everyone does?" And he say, "Pisa, you know you cannot read and I take you there for learning." That make me angry, and I say: "I speak well in many languages, and you have one language and you cannot speak it proper." Then he ask what I mean, and I say you said it. Was awful, but Pisa cannot think quick.'

I admitted that I saw how it happened, and Pisa looked so woebegone that I found myself cheering her up. But I did promise myself never again to say anything which could be repeated, which might come full circle back to me and make trouble. Although I realized at the time that that would mean I could never open my mouth except for eating and a few general comments on the weather.

That certainly was not my lucky week.

When I woke up the next morning I felt in my bones that there was worse to come.

Almost before I had reached the kitchen Mrs Aitch stepped heavily and swiftly in by the back door, which either Pisa or I had forgotten to lock the night before, making my scalp tingle with the sudden horror of her forceful entrance. She always came in as though she were taking the flat by storm and had been lying in wait for the crucial moment.

'Ho,' she said, in jolly ringing tones, 'I can see it isn't one of our good mornings. We look all washed out and no mistake.'

'And we feel all washed out.'

Mrs Aitch started to rake the boiler, putting a great deal of violent goodwill into the procedure. She made more noise than any one person who wasn't Mrs Aitch could.

I felt squalid in my dressing gown, and with my hair uncombed, but I let Mrs Aitch push me none too gently down on the kitchen stool, where I stayed, hunched up, in a state of morning collapse. I can usually pull myself together at night, no matter how late the hour; it is only in the mornings when I feel that I might easily break into a thousand pieces.

Pisa came out and joined us. The kitchen was bearable now that the boiler was going. Pisa said she would make us all some coffee.

'You do look wonderful this morning, Pisa,' I said – the words were wrung out of me. 'How do you do it?'

Pisa laughed, showing little cat teeth, very white and very shining, and her mouth was cat-pink, too. She looked so young and so well that it was hardly possible. I could not remember ever having looked as young, or as well, as that.

'Is wonderful this morning. Sunshine. You have not notice?'

'I did notice that there was a lot of light which hurt.' I felt ashamed of myself.

'Wot *you* want' – Mrs Aitch jerked her thumb at me and gave a loud coarse chuckle – 'is er man, an' wot I want is ter get rid o' mine. Twenty-five bloomin' years –'

'Well, I don't want yours, thanks very much.' I tried to enter into the playful spirit of morning banter.

'Thas the trouble,' said Mrs Aitch thoughtfully, scratching the top of her head, 'no one wants mine. A proper pest 'e is and no mistake.'

Pisa giggled and asked why. Pisa was continually fascinated by Mrs Aitch.

'Always at you the 'ole time, grabbin' and pinchin' and squeezin', and if I say ter 'im as I've said many er time, "You get off with you", 'e'll go grabbin' and pinchin' and squeezin' somewheres else.'

'But if you do not want him you are pleased that he should go. No?'

'Not on yer life.' Mrs Aitch was truculent. ''E married me an' 'e's got ter stay married, see? Otherwise I'll give 'im wot for.'

'But if you do not want him –' Pisa was puzzled.

'Ho no,' said Mrs Aitch menacingly. 'You jus' wait, my girl. When you get a man you'll want to keep 'im.'

'Now, Mrs Aitch,' I began, sternly.

'All right, all right, I'm gettin' on, aren't I? An' I'd get on quicker if you two ladies 'ud get out of me way.' Mrs Aitch managed to put the blame on Pisa and me. 'Tuctuctuc, all this cigarette ash. I don't know wot them ashtrays is for.'

When I left them Pisa was washing up the coffee cups and she and Mrs Aitch were really getting down to the subject of men, and what Mrs Aitch called 'their narsty ways', very thoroughly indeed. I only hoped that Mrs Aitch would not so far forget herself as to begin on the subject of foreigners. But Pisa, above all else good-tempered, would probably say poo, and laugh, and join in.

It must have been about eleven o'clock when Peter telephoned. I was feeling slightly more human by then – but not much.

'I say,' he said, 'I really do think you might have used a bit more finesse, you know. After all, Frederick isn't exactly one of us, is he? I mean we all kind of ganged up long before he came on the scene, and, well, it all seems pretty odd to me, and I can't get the hang of it – and now *you* –'

'Peter, what on earth are you talking about? You must be more simple and concise, especially in the morning. What have I done *now*?'

'Oh, look here, don't go on like that. Do listen for a change. This is serious. Frederick's just phoned to say that *you* don't think Alexandra ought to come out with me this evening, and I want to know why on earth not. It's no business of yours, Marianne, really it isn't. The whole thing's beyond me.'

'I don't propose that it should be my business, and the whole thing's beyond me, too. I told Frederick nothing of the kind. I said I didn't give a damn what Alexandra did, or whom she went out with. But personally I'd rather she went out with you, Peter, instead of moping at home, waiting for Frederick. Don't quote me, though. I'm not up to it.'

'That's fine;' he said, 'and I must say in all fairness Frederick didn't say *exactly* that, but that was what he gave me to understand.'

'I'm just about sick of what people give other people to understand. I've been sick of it for a long, long time, and I'm getting sicker, and I don't want to hear one word more on the subject. Is that quite clear?'

'Good Lord, you are in a huff, aren't you? After all, I did think I could talk to you. Frederick's a peculiar sort of cove, and not *our* sort, and all that, and I thought you'd been seeing him, and you'd know what he's like, and you might give me a few tips . . .' There was silence for a few seconds, then Peter asked, hesitantly: 'Has he moved in? He always seems to be there, if you know what I mean.'

'I know perfectly well what you mean, and I'm making no comment.'

'You sound like royalty. Who the hell wants you to comment? I only want a few facts.'

'Those,' I said coldly, 'are the last things which I would dream of divulging. Insinuations, maybe; conclusions, perhaps; facts, definitely not.'

'Don't be so damned clever.' Peter was obviously out of patience with me.

'I'm not at my best at this hour of the day,' I admitted. 'All I can say is I hope you both have a nice evening.'

'I'll call for Alexandra,' he said, 'whether she'll come or not.'

'That's the stuff. Bold and resolute. But haven't you told her you're calling for her?'

'I can't. Frederick always answers the phone and says she's either busy or not there.'

I had a brainwave, except, of course, that it would not work. 'Couldn't you come along, all forceful, and throw him out?'

There was a longer silence after this, while Peter let my words mill around in his mind.

'Oh, I say,' he said at last, 'but how could I? On what grounds?'

'On the grounds that you just don't like him,' I suggested.

'But Alexandra does,' he said, logically: far too logically. Obviously in Peter I had drawn a blank, and, what was much worse, Alexandra had drawn a blank, too.

'I think I'll just ignore him,' Peter said, as though he had reached a Lochinvar-like conclusion.

'That,' I said, 'would be Machiavellian.'

Peter replied that he thought there was something in it, and then rang off.

Mrs Aitch advanced with the Hoover, unemptied, as I guessed, and, as time would prove, guessed right. 'You ought to 'ave them telephones disinfected, that you ought, always at them as you are.'

I said I would think about it.

'Think, tuctuc,' said Mrs Aitch, banging the Hoover in the cupboard and then throwing her weight upon the door to get it shut. 'Do's my motto an' think afterward.'

'*You* do it for me, then. You get the telephone disinfected. Go on, do it.'

'Can't say as I've ever done it,' said Mrs Aitch, looking at me strangely.

'And I've never done it, neither,' I said crossly, talking like Mrs Aitch, as I talked like Pisa. It was such a disadvantage.

'You jus' phone someone at the 'ead and say you want them to come and do it.'

'You just come and phone someone at the head and say you want them to come and do it. It would be very nice if someone could do something for me, for a change.'

'Dear, dear, we are in a paddy,' said Mrs Aitch, backing away. 'An' that'll be one pound two and sixpence.'

'In my purse in the kitchen drawer. Help yourself.'

'An' three and eleven for me stamp.'

'In my purse. Help yourself. And, by the way, have I ever seen your card? *Do* you put the stamps on?'

'Course I do. What d'you take me for?'

'For the same as me, and I can't remember to put stamps on.'

'Fancy!' She picked her teeth with what looked like the tiny brush for cleaning out the spout of the teapot. 'Neether can I.'

I made no comment.

'Ta, and cheeribye,' she said, and went off humming 'Onward, Christian Soldiers', and I felt that we had got little, if any, further. I wondered whether she had put any stamps on her card, and added that to my list of things to 'see about' in some nebulous future.

That evening I was all alert and listening. I heard Frederick's heavy, fateful footsteps, plunging on into the darkness without a falter.

About ten minutes later there was the slurred rush of silks, the tapping of high heels, and a gentle rap on the windowpane.

Alexandra's soft voice called out, 'Night, sweetie', and I drew back the curtains and looked out on to a shimmering flurry of sequins and a smiling face framed with light-brown hair, feathered by the evening air.

'Have a lovely time,' I said, and she called back, 'Yes, I'm going to'; the car door slammed and she was gone.

I thought about the inconsistency of women; there was Alexandra, going out with Peter, who for all his hanging back was the right material for her, and yet taking him only as a second best, good for a slap-up dinner and a gay evening: with all her heart (and more, unfortunately, than her heart) given to Frederick, who was, if not exactly shoddy, something very near it.

It must have been about an hour after I had gone to bed, when I was in my first and deepest sleep, that the bell rang. When I woke myself up properly I realized that I had heard the ringing for some minutes past. Cursing everything and everybody, and hating the necessity for getting up, I dragged myself to the front door, opened it, and Alexandra threw herself in.

She looked a mess; her hair was blown about, her nose shone (as mine did, no doubt, only mine shone worse, as I had plastered my face with cold cream before going to bed), and the front of her dress was splashed with some dark stains.

'What's the matter with you *now*?' I snapped at her. It was almost intolerable to be awakened.

'It's blood;' she said, with some satisfaction, pointing to the stains on her dress. She seemed rather proud of it.

'So I can see. Have you hurt yourself?' I tried to sound sympathetic, but it was rather more than I could push myself to at that time in the morning.

'It isn't my blood, it's Frederick's.' She smiled creamily, as though the remembrance was not distasteful.

That shook me slightly, as I think she had intended.

'You haven't killed him, have you?'

She said, no, she hadn't, and then she began to laugh, not hysterically, but a genuine, soft, amused laughter.

'It's all very well,' I said, 'but what about me? You can't come in here, just laughing around the place, covered with blood, at this time in the morning. What on earth is all this about?' I wished that Alexandra would go back to her own flat and look after her own life. The young, and their problems, and their scenes, and their minds not made up, or, more likely, their minds just not being used, become so tiring that one longs for nothing except sleep, and for all of them to go away and to keep very, very quiet.

She stood and stared at me with large, deer-like, accusing eyes.

'Oh, come in, if you must. You'll have to sit in the bedroom, that's the only place that's moderately warm. And you can get yourself a glass of milk – oh, and get me one too, will you?'

Alexandra trotted off, and returned with two large mugs of milk.

'You get back into bed, darling,' she said, 'then we can talk.'

'Must we talk *now*? Must we really?'

'Well, I do think you're unkind. Here I am, covered with blood, and you don't really care. Aren't you a bit interested in what's happened?'

'Of course I'm interested.' Then I asked her, somewhat sharply, whether she had had a lot to drink. I thought her words were slightly slurred, and I could imagine a whole evening spent in Peter's company, sentimental and nostalgic, and drinking their way through it, and talking in nebulous terms of what might have been.

'I'll tell you what we've been drinking,' Alexandra said

bitterly. 'Mead – and it's filthy, like old cabbage water with honey in it, and you have to drink it out of beakers; don't ask me why, it's just a custom, and never let it be said that one does not follow the custom. Filthy. Of course, it may have gone off.'

'But what about all that blood?'

'Darling, I've got to tell it in my way, or not at all.'

I sat back and tried to compose myself patiently.

'Well, first the dinner – and what a dinner. If only I could have had the food spread over a week, but for one evening it was literally monstrous.'

'That doesn't move me,' I said. 'I could probably eat it all, this very minute.'

'We drove for miles, Epping, Elstree or somewhere,' she continued, taking no notice. 'It was supposed to be a Tudor dinner, and no wonder they died young. Halfway through I thought I'd pass out with the sheer agony of it; swan and peacock and crane pie, and flummery, and little candied bits and pieces that tasted of syrup of figs, and all through it beakers and beakers of that awful mead. To add to the general strangeness, a peculiar-looking creature poured into a doublet and baggy knickers came and squatted at my feet and twanged away at some rude instrument, made from two strings stretched over a bit of wood. And no coffee because that would have been out of keeping, and no smoking because it hadn't been invented, and candles stuck into lumps of twisted metal, and the kind of candles that drip incessantly ... What with the peacock, the pie, the mead, the smell of candle-grease, and the eunuch twanging around my feet, I've never felt quite so odd in my life before. You have to throw the mead down your throat because those beastly beakers are so authentic that if you try to sip the stuff it just pours all over you.'

'Such absolutely authentic discomfort must have cost quite a packet,' I said.

'Fabulous. Of course, I had to make some return for all that lavishing, so I listened for hours and hours while Peter talked about himself, and the shameful thing is, considering all that money, and all that time, I can't really remember what he did say. He told me so much and in such appalling detail that it washed over me. The general gist was that whatever was wrong with him wasn't his fault –'

'And what *is* wrong with him?'

'Practically everything, but I gather he's going to have himself put right, and once you're properly put right you're much righter than anyone who hasn't been wrong to start with.'

'That will be something to look forward to.'

'That's more or less what I said, but it didn't seem to be the answer he wanted. Apparently he thought I was no end mean not to appreciate all the trouble he's taking to get himself put right.'

'That sounds a familiar theme,' I said. 'But what about the blood?'

'We're not nearly there yet. You simply must get the general atmosphere.'

I yawned and pushed the pillows into the small of my back. It was obviously going to be a long session.

'I said but surely he wanted to be put right for his own sake, and he said not particularly, having been wrong for so long he'd almost stopped noticing. But he'd go through with being put right if it would lead to something. And then he asked me to marry him. I told him I thought it was a pity he hadn't asked me before, but now there was Frederick. Then Peter swore a lot, but quite softly and sadly, and of course by then I was quite emotional what with the mead and everything – and I cried large tears into my flummery, and the eunuch, who, believe it or not, had been huddled at my feet the whole time, began to make simply heart-rending noises on the two strings, and we had quite a little crying jag, all three of us. The eunuch wept quietly in my lap, and Peter blew his nose and mopped his eyes over some subtle confection of chestnuts swimming in fermented honey, and I soaked the flummery, and, d'you know, not a soul seemed to notice – or perhaps they just didn't care.'

'Maybe mead takes people that way,' I suggested.

'Mead or not, it was all most frightfully sad, and yet somehow impersonal, as though we were all crying because of everything – as I suppose we were – at least *I* was, because I've got Frederick, so there really wasn't anything for me to cry about – except having eaten too much, and having no money, and large things which are far too awful to cry about, such as the hydrogen bomb . . . Anyway, we all wept our way through and finished up quite cheerful, because I remember that we all kissed each other, rather like the Chelsea Arts Ball used to be – and then, I think, we were put out, oh, ever so politely, but without reprieve, and Peter said what would I like to do *now*, so I said coffee, very black, so we drove back to his flat. And Peter kept on saying what a fool he'd been, and I said I ought not to see him again because of Frederick.'

'You are absurd, Alexandra, to dramatize everything like that.'

'Peter quite saw the point; he said he had decided after all not to get himself put right, because it wouldn't be worth it. Just when we were settled down there was a dreadful hammering on the door. And Peter said, "Don't let's take any notice. It's only the old soak upstairs. No one else comes at this hour, but if he sees a light he always tries it on in the hope of getting one last snifter." Of course I agreed fervently, especially as I felt nearly dead. Anyone would be laid out by that dinner – I don't know why people do it, except, of course, that it's the thing at the moment and chic, and so on, otherwise no one would do it for pleasure, would they?'

'It's a compliment,' I said. 'Being bought something expensive always is, especially if it is something one doesn't want. But what *happened*?'

'The hammering went on quite relentlessly, and just when Peter was hauling himself up there was a shocking noise of smashing and destruction, and, what d'you think? Frederick had actually broken in – but literally. There's a thick glass pane in the door and he'd just put his hand through it. He came stamping in looking extremely ridiculous, of course, as people always do when they do ridiculous things and make large gestures, but I wouldn't have minded that so much if there hadn't been blood dripping everywhere. My first reaction was that I wished I had done it to him and not let him do it to himself. All very unworthy, no doubt, but there it is. One just isn't worthy more often than not.'

'What *did* you do?' I asked, wondering what one would do in such a situation, and coming to no conclusion.

'I'm mortified to have to admit that what with the sight of blood, which turns me up, and the dinner, and the mead, and the utter abortiveness of the whole evening, I lost my head completely and I just jumped up and down and screamed. If only I could have it all over again – although God forbid, but what I mean is, if only I could have it again, not having had it once, but being prepared for it – well, then I'd behave with such dignity. What made me good and mad, of course, was the melodrama about nothing. It was just banal and in extremely bad taste.'

'What did Frederick say?' I rather liked the idea of Frederick having hurt himself badly, but I realized that he hadn't hurt himself all that badly, which was practically unforgivable.

'He bellowed a lot at first in an animalish kind of way, but that wasn't exactly saying anything – at least if he did it was lost on me, because anyway I was making far too much noise myself by then and I could only hear myself, and what I was saying wasn't interesting. He just stood there, dripping blood, until Peter fetched a towel, and with Frederick's hand and arm swathed in a towel the whole thing became terribly Roman. And then, and this is what really got me, Peter turned upon me, *me*, and shouted at me to keep quiet. And then, what do you think?'

I shook my head numbly; I was past thinking.

'Well, Frederick roared vituperations and all against me, *not* at Peter, and Peter said he could quite understand, and started to soothe Frederick, and to commiserate with him, saying what a dreadful time he must have had both before and during and after he put his fist through the glass. They got so matey you just wouldn't believe it.'

I said that I could believe anything of either of them, and also said, not, I think, for the first time: 'You do pick them, don't you?'

'I don't pick them at all, I never have. *They* pick me. I seem to be everybody's pawn, and I'm more than sick of it. I used to be a moderately nice young woman, but niceness doesn't pay, and although I haven't yet discovered what does pay, once I know niceness doesn't, then niceness is out. From now on I'm going to smash and grab, too. There won't be any more of "After you, sir, and let me await your august pleasure", you can be sure of that.'

'More or less the same thoughts have occurred to me, from

time to time,' I admitted. 'And although they do no good, and they aren't exactly constructive, yet it's a comfort to think them ... But how did you end up? What chaos or camaraderie have you left behind?'

'Oh, both. Peter brought out some port, because evidently he hadn't anything else, or did not want to produce what else he had, which is more likely.'

That sounded authentic. Even in a crisis Peter was capable of considering what would be the best for him in the long run.

'And there we sat, drinking port, and Frederick continued to drip through the folds of the towel which wasn't all that cunningly arranged, and Peter kept on saying how well he understood – and even Frederick became a trifle baffled by Peter's all-embracing understanding, and all I gathered was that Frederick had the effrontery – and lack of comprehension of human motives – to think that I had gone back with Peter because I was up to no good. That's the point: it wasn't *Peter* who was up to no good, it was me. And Peter kept on saying, "I do see, old chap, I really do, and Alexandra ought to have explained how you'd feel, and I'd never have brought her back here", and I could have screamed all over again, and I'm not sure that I didn't, and thinking back I hope I did. And I kept on saying to Frederick: "What about your hand? Do you want to bleed to death? Is that your idea of fun?" And he just looked pale and tortured, and *he* kept on saying that he was all right, and then he swayed a little, to show how far from all right he was. I really hated him then, just for a few seconds, anyway. It all seemed such a monstrous act, except for the blood which was real enough.'

'Coming back to everyday matters, wouldn't it be a good idea if you went into the kitchen and mopped some of that blood off?'

'Why?' Alexandra lit another cigarette. 'You don't think that I'm ever going to wear this dress again, do you? I'd rather die than put it on. I shall burn it.'

'Not now,' I said quickly, in case she translated this into immediate action – she was capable of it. 'It isn't necessary to go to such lengths, and besides, the smell would be awful.'

'Don't you want to hear the end of it?'

'Yes, but do hurry up. I can't keep awake much longer.' An engulfing wave of tiredness came over me.

'Well, I left them there, and they didn't even try to stop me. They were sitting close as close and agreeing how insensitive women were. Just before I left I actually heard Peter say, all low and heartfelt, that Frederick might find I'd get upset again, either later tonight, or in the morning, and he must try to be patient with me. Now what do you think of *that*?'

'That was certainly forbidding,' I said, and yawned again.

'And if Frederick's hand is badly cut he won't be able to work for weeks, and he probably won't go to a doctor until his whole arm is infected and swells up, and *that* will be my fault, too.'

'Couldn't you have poured some disinfectant over it? That might have been a double pleasure – it would have hurt horribly and might have stopped the gangrene or whatever it is.'

'I wasn't sufficiently pulled together, and I didn't care what happened to either of them. I'm only realizing, now, what might result. Can't you just see Frederick tucked up in bed in my flat, and me fetching and carrying for him, and Peter visiting him and peeling grapes and popping them in his mouth? Very touching.'

'Well, I must say it seems to have brought you back to your senses, which is something.'

'It isn't exactly the way I'd choose – just you try eating

mounds of spiced swan and drinking cabbage water, and then having someone break through a door and come in dripping blood and splash it all over you – *and* accompanied by a lot of nonsense about purity and faithfulness into the bargain. I'm beyond being lectured about behaving properly. Let other people behave properly, just for a change.'

'Yes,' I said, 'I think you've got something there. But what are you going to do now? This very minute?'

She screwed her nose up and looked puckered, perplexed, and very tired; suddenly very tired.

'Frederick's still got a frightful hold on me. I don't like it. It isn't real; at least if it is real, then it oughtn't to be. But he *has* got a hold, mostly physical, becoming habitual, which is the most dangerous of all, although men don't realize it, and insist on regarding habit as an insult, but that's because they're more romantic, taken by and large, than we are. I'm getting so used to having him there.'

'That's what he banked on when he moved in,' I said. 'What's more important is, can you get used to *not* having him there?'

She was silent for a minute, obviously taking herself to task.

'I could think myself out of it, if I tried hard enough. I must have thought myself into it, in the first place.'

'That's a clever girl,' I said. 'And while you're thinking I'll put some rugs and pillows on the sofa and you can sleep on that. If you want to get away from Frederick you must make yourself inaccessible, then he'll move out. There's no other way. Otherwise when he comes back, as I suppose he will, he'll begin all over again, and he'll shout at you, and you'll cry, and then he'll tell you the cut just missed the vein, but only just, and in the end you'll throw yourselves exhausted into each other's arms. And you'll find yourself apologizing to him. I know it all. It's a very familiar routine. But if that's what you want, go to it. I'm not trying to stop you.'

'By the time you've put the rugs and pillows out I'll have made up my mind.'

'Oh no, you don't.' I was exasperated. 'You make up your mind now. I'm not lugging in rugs and pillows to try to turn a sofa into a bed if you're not going to sleep on it.'

'All right,' said Alexandra, suddenly defeated by herself. 'I'll go back and wait for Frederick to come in, and everything will begin all over again, and I'm a fool.'

'If that's how you want it,' I said. 'You haven't really altered much, have you?'

'No, and I don't suppose I shall now.'

Meekly Alexandra kissed me goodnight, and took herself off upstairs.

Not all my talk could accomplish what Pisa could do so very easily; just by a bright glance and a slim rounded arm waving through a window.

I had seen neither Alexandra nor Frederick for two days. I began to wonder whether they had died up there, clenched in an eternal embrace. It might have suited Frederick very well, if only he could have returned to view his own grand gesture. But as it really would be the end I thought it was safe to assume that he would boggle at it. To make sure, I did creep upstairs to see whether the milk had been taken in. It had. Then I knew that after a day spent 'having it out' they were probably sleeping it off.

What a life, I thought, and I was glad that apart from Pisa, who did not count intimately, I lived alone. It was better so.

On the third morning it happened. I had to go out early to deliver to a film studio the typed synopsis of a film which, most likely, would never be made, and if it were made then the studio ought to be thoroughly ashamed of itself. It was already a day late and the executives (they always call themselves this) had decided to have an extraordinary board meeting to discuss the synopsis of the film, the story of which, in broad outline, had only been made into a film five or six times before – so the whole matter was very urgent. So urgent – especially as I was getting paid on the dot, and it might lead to my being asked to type other synopses of other films which would never be made – that I decided to sacrifice myself to art, and go out before breakfast.

I explained the position to Pisa, who said that it was very fonny to want to make films so early in the morning, and she would prepare breakfast and have it ready for me by the time I came back. I began to see what Alexandra meant about not wanting to live alone. The realization that when I returned Pisa would be there, with coffee and croissants, and pretty little curls of butter, and an absurd but gay little linen traycloth carefully placed on the one tray which is quite presentable without a cloth, and all the wrong cups and saucers and plates, and the wrong knives, too, and the coffee made in a pot which no one but Pisa would think of using on which is written *A Present from Brighton* – well, remembering all these homely comforts, the excursion did not seem quite so intolerable after all.

When I got back, Pisa was flushed and starry-eyed; flushed, as I supposed, from a hot bath, and starry-eyed just because she was Pisa.

The coffee tasted good; the croissants were crisp and hot; and I began to think that this going out before breakfast might, if I could keep it up, be my salvation. But the intoxicated mood soon faded and I became myself again.

Pisa was very breathless and excited, but she knew that the mornings weren't my best times, and she kept quiet until I had finished my second cup of coffee.

'Pisa has very fonny news,' she said. 'You like to hear?'

I nodded. 'If it isn't too long and complicated.'

'Very simple,' said Pisa, dimpling. 'Is this. I go and bathe, and when I want to come out to prepare breakfast the door stick, as it often stick, and will not open. I could not begin to open, for the key will not turn the lock. Is often so. Not?'

'Not,' I said. 'At least not in my experience. Why didn't you tell me there was something wrong with the lock?'

'I do not tell not to trouble you. I think, too, that you will know, being your key and your lock, and to myself I say, it is always the same in England, being the dampness of the atmosphere. So I say nothing.'

'Surely,' I said, 'it isn't only in England that there is dampness in the atmosphere in a bathroom? It must be pretty general.'

'Please? But I do not make myself clear. In England you have the dampness inside and the dampness outside, making two dampnesses meeting, which is different from my country, being only the one dampness from the inside where the hot water has collected in steam drops –'

'Yes, yes, I see,' I interrupted hastily, wishing that I had not brought up the point.

'So I take hold of the key, like this' – Pisa demonstrated with both hands, as though the key were about a foot long and several inches thick – 'and I pull and I pull, and I go this way and I go that way, and I lean the door in and I push the door out, but nothing move. So I start to sweat and begin to feel the fright coming and I say to myself how long will I live there, not being enough air, as when the fright come I breathe very fast and use up air. But when I feel that I swoon and my eyes sweat and I cannot see to hold the key any more, I hear footsteps walking out the garden way, and you guess whose they are, walking out the garden way –'

Pisa paused, all tense and excited, obviously reliving her own drama with great enjoyment.

'You tell me,' I said.

'You must guess,' Pisa pouted. 'You make just one tiny guess.'

I tried hard. 'The milkman?' I suggested.

'Poo,' she said contemptuously. 'The milkman! He does not come the garden way. You do not try. It was Frederick!' She was evidently very pleased about this, although I could not think why.

'What did you do?' I asked, obediently, although I could not be expected to work myself up about the possibility of Pisa's passing out from lack of air in the bathroom. There was a small but perfectly workable window which could be opened and shut with the minimum of effort, through which Pisa could obtain enough air to enable her to breathe as hard as she liked for as long as she lived. I still didn't see what this was leading up to.

'So I am weak, but I push myself to the window which is open one tiny piece' – Pisa demonstrated again, impressing upon me the desperateness of her situation – 'and I get out my hand, but only to my wrist, and I cry, "Help, help! I am not able to open the door –"'

Pisa paused dramatically.

'How did you know it was Frederick?' I asked. 'You couldn't see him, could you?'

'But no. I hear him by the steps of his walk.'

'Did you now?' It was beginning to get interesting. Pisa

had obviously been lying in wait for Frederick. I had the glimmering of an idea, but I did not want to promise myself too much.

'So I cry "Help, help!",' Pisa took up the saga, 'and Frederick bend down and look in a tiny piece, but that I am not able to stop, being swooned, and Frederick say, "What has happen?" And I say, very faint, "Is Pisa, and Pisa is prisoner as the door is sticked", and he say, "If you will try to get the key and bring and put through window I will come and let you out, if I can get in". And I say, "Yes, you get in as kitchen door not closed".' Pisa paused again, slightly breathless, and looking very very pleased with herself. 'So he do that, and I say, it is naughty being swooned after my bathe, but Frederick say it is not naughty, for I would die if he did not come then. Is fonny, no?'

'Very funny, but quite nicely funny,' I said, and I smiled at her, and she smiled back at me, knowingly, and blushed slightly.

'And that is not all. The large surprise makes me sad for leaving you, because we are friends, and I am so happy. But I must leave without saying one word. I am not able to explain. I will write, I will write much, and when I have money I will pay you for your goodness and for all you do for me, and soon I come back to visit and we make your clothes all new and very smart. No?'

I began to see the light, or I hoped I did.

'Pisa dear, you don't have to repay me for anything. I've enjoyed your being here, and I mean that. I think I understand, and I won't say a word to anyone, not even Alexandra, especially not Alexandra. Is that right?'

Pisa nodded, and looked down at her feet. 'Is awful?' she asked happily. 'Is shameful?'

'I don't know. Perhaps it is awful and shameful, but I think you can cope better than Alexandra can.'

'Please?' Pisa asked appealingly, then said: 'He was mine. He was not hers. Now I get him back, and we go away.'

'You'd better go away soon, hadn't you?'

'Immediate.' Pisa beamed. 'I pack. You permit?'

'But certainly,' I said. 'I'll come and help you.'

'Is not necessary, I thank you. I have almost pack. Is damn exciting, no?'

I agreed that it was damn exciting. 'How long have you been working up to this?'

I thought that Pisa would pretend that she didn't understand, but perhaps she decided there was no need.

'From when I meet him,' she said with dignity. 'Pisa knows what she wants.'

I regarded her with growing admiration. She certainly did know what she wanted, and had an aptitude for getting it, which is rare. That what she wanted should happen to be what I was anxious to be rid of was, naturally, greatly in her favour.

'What about Frederick? How will he manage to pack? He might be – well, hindered . . . I mean he might not get through as soon as you expect.'

'Poo,' she said. 'Is his business, not Pisa's.'

'That's the way,' I said. 'You just go on remembering that.' Quite obviously Frederick had met his match.

'Frederick work,' Pisa said proudly. 'Frederick work damn hard. We open shop. Sell sausage, black bread, coffee, good coffee. Very dear, but good, all very good.'

'How will you get the money? You can't open a shop without any money.'

'Frederick write his damn silly book, and quick,' she said,

firmly. 'I stand by him, and he write. If he do not write he do not eat. If he do not write for long I do not eat neither. He write. You see. I say to him, you finish damn silly book quick, and he promise. And until he finish there is much to sell. He has gold buttons in his shirt sleeves, and a watch from America that tells time and date and rings a bell. We get plenty for them until he write book. You see.'

I was dumb with admiration. How easy it all was.

I realized that there was no mention of Frederick's being faint from loss of blood, or having his arm in a sling, but perhaps Pisa, with an eye only to the main chance, just failed to notice any irrelevant details.

'I think I'd rather happen to be out and to find you gone when I return. Would you mind?' I asked.

'But that is best. You go away, and you come back, and I leave note saying goodbye, and you show note, and everyone is happy. No?'

'Well, everyone won't be happy straight away,' I said. 'But soon, very soon.'

After Pisa made her announcement I took myself off as quickly and as quietly as possible. What does one do with oneself at that time of day, when one simply cannot go home? I walked around for half an hour or so, and felt very virtuous, taking such unaccustomed exercise twice in one morning. But that soon palled. Then I went into a café and had a cup of coffee, but one cannot sit alone over a cup of coffee for long – at least I can't. So I made my way towards the Tube station and bought a lunchtime racing edition of an evening paper, which led me into backing two horses. One came in last and the other fell.

Then I looked at my wristwatch and saw that I had only been out an hour. Not long enough.

So I took another little walk, and thought how remarkably ugly all the houses were.

I could imagine Pisa, brisk and bright and very efficient, running an espresso bar. I could see her, smiling beguilingly, beribboned and shining as ever, carefully nurturing her charmingly foreign accent, turning her phrases round and about, and, most musically, never getting her grammar right. And Frederick? Oh yes, Frederick would do his stuff excellently: Pisa would see to that. Looking so tall, well built, fair-haired, with such true grey eyes, how could he fail? He would become a local showpiece; such a nice chap, not quite the type for that kind of thing, d'you think? Once that got around, he'd be made. Pisa would make herself, anyway. But I could see Frederick, not doing a great deal, but looking so staunch and reliable, leaning over the counter, talking to one or two regulars, while Pisa flipped and flapped prettily, doing most of the work, but making a play of it.

Now and again she would order him about, enchanting everyone with a great display of mock severity. And Frederick would smile indulgently, and make soft-voiced affectionate comments on what it was to be married to such a virago of a woman. He would often refer to 'my wife', in a lazily loving way, and everyone would say: 'But aren't they absolutely sweet together? Of course, he just adores her.'

And he had better continue to adore her. Pisa would stand no nonsense. And that, too, was exactly what Frederick needed.

After the café-bar had closed, no matter how tired she might be, Pisa would check through the accounts. Through and through until they balanced to the last penny. And Frederick would sigh and yawn, and stand first on one leg, then on the other, but he would have to wait until the accounts came right.

In ten or fifteen years' time, when, by Pisa's unremitting efforts, they had saved up enough, Pisa would sell the espresso, at a substantial profit, and, taking Frederick with her, as part of the luggage of her life, would transport them both to Italy, where, perhaps, she would negotiate for the purchase of a smallholding, which would include the traditional few acres of olive trees and vineyards; which, labour being cheap and easily obtainable, she would run with the minimum of effort and expense. And there, at last, Frederick could go to pieces, could run contentedly to seed, as he had long dreamed of doing. He could spend his mornings at the local café, swilling down Americanos, his afternoons asleep, and his evenings in the same café, drinking Tia Maria, and telling everyone who would listen, or who would pretend to listen, how he had given up his academic career, thrown away the promise of a fellowship, to marry Pisa.

To make up for all he was not, he would continue, perhaps to the end of his life, to be superbly satisfactory in bed. Not that Pisa would care greatly, but if he expended himself on her he would have little to spare for anyone else; which would be all to the good.

... But that still left me with another hour to fritter away before it was safe for me to go home. I could not risk arriving in the middle of their departure and becoming even more deeply involved.

So I chose a side-street restaurant and ate my way wretchedly through a three-and-ninepenny luncheon. Never again. By then I had done my penance and could allow myself to return.

I slunk in as quietly as possible, just in case Alexandra was on the look out for me, and I realized, immediately, that the flat was different. A certain scent of someone being there, someone else, had gone. Or, perhaps, I knew that it had gone, otherwise I might not have noticed.

What was impossible not to notice was a large empty space in the hall; Pisa had evidently made expeditious arrangements for Mrs Vassenheimer's machine to be returned. How I had cursed the thing, and how I wished it back, representing, as it had done, the security of a familiar background, of familiar sounds, of the bustle of life continuing. Yes, some part of life had gone, and Pisa had taken it with her. I remembered how wary, how ill-at-ease, I had felt, when first she had announced her intention of arriving – never did I think that I would wish her back so desperately.

Desperately? Then I began to realize what Alexandra must be feeling. It is not the worth of the person, but the amount which one loses by the loss, which counts. Perhaps for the very first time I realized that. I realized, too, every trifling unrecorded gesture, every turn of head, every footstep, which Alexandra would wait for, and find wanting. And I began, too late, alas, as it usually is, to wish Frederick back, worthless as I felt sure he was, but worth whatever price Alexandra might put upon him.

Suddenly I was frightened. She was young; impetuous; easily thrown off her balance; suffering from the daze of first love; beginning to bed herself down in a soft and sensuous relationship; accepting both the tension and the mistrust because, by hard and difficult roads, they led to a piercing point of joy, although they might (which she had not yet discovered, and now would never discover), if all else were incompatible, lead nowhere else at all. And what might she not do now, with all these newfound delights snatched from her?

What, in heaven's name, did it matter what *I* thought about Frederick?

And I promised myself that I would, from that time on, remain a spectator, and never allow myself to become too much a part of the lives of other people. I haven't entirely succeeded – but, given time, I shall. And if time is taken from me first, remember that I would have succeeded – given time.

After all this I decided to go to Alexandra, and to present myself, however inopportunely, to see whether what was so wrong could be made, at least to some small extent, right again.

There was no sound from her flat, and when I rang the doorbell the very ringing echoed as though the flat were empty.

After a few minutes there was a faint scratching on the inside of the door and a low, gruff purr.

'Oh, Tom,' I said, 'I'm so glad you're there.' And so I was, because I knew that Alexandra would come back. She wouldn't leave Tom. She wouldn't leave a stupid good-for-nothing cat like that.

Then I heard footsteps come wearily towards me, and Alexandra opened the door.

Her face was swollen and blotched from crying, and she clutched in her hand a little screwed-up fragment of paint rag, all damp and useless.

'And I've even run out of handkerchiefs,' were the first words she said to me. 'Isn't that quite the end!'

I fished in my handbag and found a clean one, all neat and folded, and gave it to her.

She thanked me, and blew her nose, then polished the tip, as she usually did, and said: 'Do come in, and forgive me, I look such a sight. Don't worry, I've finished crying. I've cried myself out, and I've got a simply ghastly headache and my eyes feel as though they've been boiled.'

I followed her into the flat, while Tom weaved in and out our legs, showing, perhaps for the first time, some proper cat feelings and animation. I thought it was just like him to choose such a crisis to behave as any self-respecting cat should; perhaps the only day on which no one cared.

The flat was in an awful muddle, worse than I had ever seen it. Alexandra was fairly fussy about her small number of possessions, and her only untidiness was the cosy confusion of work. But this was different. Everything was strewn about, tossed aside, crooked and sad-looking.

'In case you don't know,' Alexandra said in a muted voice, 'although I'm fairly sure you do, Frederick has gone. He won't ever come back, either. Doesn't that please you?'

'Not particularly,' I said. 'Not now.'

'So it would have pleased you yesterday, or the day before, or the day before that, but it doesn't please you now?'

'Yes,' I said. 'That's just it, more or less.'

We sat in a stunned silence for a few seconds.

'I'm terribly sorry,' I said, 'not about Frederick, but about you, feeling as you so obviously do. But it really wasn't my doing, although you might think so.'

'Yes, at first I did think so, but afterwards I knew it wasn't. You wouldn't bother, would you? Not either way?'

'No, I wouldn't bother. But what I have done is to do nothing at all. I didn't try to stop it. Not that I could have.'

'For God's sake get some pleasure out of it, can't you? You hated Frederick, and you did everything you could to make things go wrong between us, and now everything has gone wrong, for ever, you can't even be glad. I think that's downright mean.'

'I didn't hate Frederick, I just didn't like him.'

'*I* didn't like him, either. I didn't even know him – he was always putting on an act. He wasn't even truthful, not even in everyday factual matters. All that guff about the grant wasn't true, to begin with. He'd got one, all right, but not for as long as he pretended, not until he'd finished his thesis or whatever it was. Only for the first year, to see how he made out. If he'd produced a promising beginning, just that, they'd have given him the whole damn shoot, and he could have stayed here another five years, if he'd wanted to. He couldn't even do that. He had nothing to show – nothing. He just mooned around pretending to take notes, pretending he was going to do this, that and the other. Even *that* didn't matter. I guessed it, anyway. He was a sponger and a liar and he hadn't much talent, but I enjoyed every minute I was with him, except those minutes when I was so sick I could have killed myself. But those were soon over, and the rest of it was worth all the dreadfulnesses, and I wouldn't have minded taking every scrap of the bad, because of the good which I wanted. Frederick always said you were jealous, and you'd do all you could to muck it up.'

'Did you believe him?' I asked, as calmly as I could.

'No, I didn't. *That* was one of his dreadfulnesses, too, but I let him say it, although it was against you, and I wouldn't let anyone else say anything against you. But I let him say it because I knew it didn't mean anything, except for the second, and it wasn't worth arguing about.'

'You'd have had a shocking life, the two of you together, anyway.' That I could not resist.

'Now *I* shall have a shocking life, the two of us apart. Is that preferable?'

I did not reply because there seemed nothing left to say. In one way Alexandra was being monstrously unfair; in another she wasn't. It always comes down to that, and most matters cancel themselves out.

'I suppose you know about Pisa?' Alexandra asked. 'Oh, don't worry, he was quite explicit. I suppose because he knew she was there, all ready to fight for him. Not that she was ever put to the test. But *did* you know?'

I told her, briefly, what Pisa had told me.

'The bitch,' she said.

'But then in his way Frederick was a bitch, too – there's just no other word.'

'Yes,' she said, 'I suppose he was, and I suppose he still is, and I suppose he always will be.'

'You were so different from anyone else,' I said, 'and I expect you put him into a delightful bewilderment. But when he came to, he realized that Pisa was the type of woman he could understand. The kind of woman who could cope with him, and not make a lifetime's work out of it, either. She'll cope with him as a sideline, and continue the business of her life unimpeded.'

'Whereas now *I* can continue the business of my life unimpeded,' Alexandra said sharply. 'And I hope that satisfies all of you.'

'What do you mean, all of us?'

'Do you really think I don't know what's been going on? Chatter, chatter, chatter, all around me. Why, it's nearly driven me mad. And it's nearly driven Frederick mad, too.'

'What on earth are you talking about?'

'There's Marius, for one. He told me that he had to tell you that he was, as he put it, on our side. Why would he have made such a point of telling you that unless *you* were definitely *not* on our side?'

I didn't reply.

'Never mind, never mind. I've said enough, you've said enough, we've all said enough. And as we can't seem to keep away from the subject, perhaps it might be as well if we didn't see each other for a while. I'm sorry, but *I* simply can't cope. Maybe Pisa can, but I can't. Oh, there's just one thing. Would you be kind enough to look after Tom, just for tonight? I can't cope with him, either, and he hasn't eaten. I've arranged for Mrs Aitch to come in tomorrow morning and put the place to rights, so before she goes she can come and collect Tom, if that's all right with you?'

Feeling much shattered, I said yes, I would look after Tom, and as I was on the ground floor he wouldn't need his box because he could prowl around in the yard.

Tom, mistakenly thinking that life was running its normal course for the three of us, had gone back to sleep again. I picked him up and put him over my shoulder, where he stayed, supine, unnoticing. Alexandra turned her back purposefully upon me, and I went off, miserably, wearing Tom like a peculiar fur necklet.

When I got back to my flat I opened a tin of crayfish, which had not been one of my most inspired purchases, and coaxed Tom to eat. In the end he pecked a little, but his heart wasn't in it. After that I took him out into the yard, but he didn't seem to care for that, either. Then he came and slept on the sofa while I did some typing.

At last, and how long it seemed, the evening came, and I could draw the curtains, and shut out the dank air and the bleak grey half-light. Then I prepared sardines on toast, which Tom condescended to share with me; then we went to bed. Tom slept on my feet.

When I awoke in the morning Tom wasn't there. He had got out of the window and was sitting, cross and bedraggled, in the yard. He walked in, slowly, obviously ill-at-ease. He stared at me with an expression of animal resignation.

Alexandra was right. He had a very special cat face. Not entirely pleasing, but forceful. He accepted some milk and sipped a little, but pleasurelessly. Then he cleaned his back leg thoroughly, and, having tired himself out, jumped on the draining-board and went soundly to sleep. Maybe he liked it there, or at any rate disliked it least there. I prepared breakfast around him, and missed Pisa all over again. Besides, it would be a long time before I could forget her: all my clothes were still extremely tight. Pisa had said that they would 'ease themselves to me', but she was wrong there.

About ten o'clock Mrs Aitch came to collect Tom.

By then I had managed to get dressed, but nothing else was done.

'Tuctuc,' said Mrs Aitch reprovingly, taking it all in: the unwashed breakfast dishes, the unswept floor, the general air of defeat. '*We're* in a fine old mess too this morning, aren't we? Like me ter give you an 'and?'

I said yes, I would very much like that. Mrs Aitch helped herself to a cigarette and said, 'Ta', then she lit mine and pocketed the matches.

'I fergot ter mention last time something's got itself caught in the snake.'

'*What* snake?'

'Why, the snake that's put on the vacuum ter get the bits from corners.'

Mrs Aitch went and fetched the snake, a long rubberized instrument like an elephant's trunk.

'D'you actually *use* the thing?' I asked.

''Course I do. Wot d'you take me for? Loony?'

There certainly was something caught in the snake. When shaken it rattled.

'One o' that foreigner's bobbins or whatever they're called,

I expect. An' now I come ter think of it, wot's 'appened ter that great thing in the 'all she's forever playin' at?'

'It's gone,' I said. 'So has Pisa. She was only staying here until she found somewhere else.'

'Makin' a convenience of you,' said Mrs Aitch, wrestling with the snake, and at last managing to get some piece unscrewed, although I don't know whether that was her intention. Then she thrust her solid freckled arm up the opening and drew out pins and hair clips and multitudinous odds and ends. The whole conglomeration turned my stomach.

'Got it,' she said triumphantly. 'A fair muck in there.'

'Wouldn't it have been better if you'd put some newspapers down before you started on your excavations?'

''Course it would, and so I would've done if I'd known anything 'ud come of it. That's better, though; you sound more yourself, telling me off. Thought you were too milk and water ter live long this mornin' and no mistake.'

'So did I,' I said, feeling much recovered.

'Doesn't do ter let people get you down, an' I know what I'm talkin' about. My, you nearly 'ad me over, Tom. What's that cat doin' 'ere? 'E belongs upstairs, don't 'e?'

'Yes, but Miss Alexandra wasn't feeling well and I said I'd have him for one night. You remember, don't you, you came to take him back?'

''Course I did. Got an 'ead like a sieve, always 'ave 'ad. My dad used ter say . . . all right, no need ter look black at me. I'm gettin' on, aren't I? . . . It do seem funny, though, don't it, both o' them pushin' off, that Pessoo or whatever she called 'erself, an' that man upstairs. Almost look like they knew what they was doin', don't it? An' don't you make that face at me. I've got a right to think same as anyone, an' what I think I say.'

'Well, don't say it anywhere else, will you?'

"'Course I won't. What d'you take me for? A bloody old gossip? ... Now, a bit more shipshape, aren't we? Same time Sat'day?'

She helped herself to another cigarette, said, 'Ta, and cheeribye', and jaunted off.

After she had been gone for about five minutes I realized that she had forgotten about Tom, and I had forgotten to remind her.

So I decided to take him up myself.

I found Alexandra packing.

'I thought I told Mrs Aitch to bring Tom up? I hope he wasn't a nuisance.'

'No, he wasn't a nuisance, but I don't think he liked it much.'

'Now you are here you might as well sit down.'

I sat down.

'I'm going to stay with my aunt for a week or two. The one who lived in Tunbridge Wells, but doesn't now, she's moved to Brighton.'

'What about Tom? Wouldn't you like me to keep him?'

'No, thanks. I've told her I'm bringing a large, quiet cat. I've got to lug his box along, too, which is a bit of a bind.'

'Can't you get him another down there?'

'It may be this box or the carpet with a cat like Tom.'

'What will you take him in?'

'Oh, he'll travel in the basket he came in. Almost the size of a house. I'll have to tip everyone madly all the time. Can you lend me a pound? I'll send it back to you.'

I said, of course I could, as though there had never been a time when I couldn't.

'If you hadn't brought Pisa into this house this wouldn't have happened.'

'Perhaps,' I said. 'But if you hadn't given a party and invited Bernhardt, then *he* wouldn't have brought Pisa along in the first place, and so on, and so on.'

'Oh, do stop it! I know, I know, and if Peter hadn't got himself shut in the garage and caught a cold ... We could go on like this for ever. But what really started the rot was my going out with Peter that evening, and then Frederick putting his hand through the glass. I don't think he ever properly forgave me for that, and that *was* your fault.'

Then I lost my temper, and we both said the same things over again, but much more heatedly.

Then Alexandra cried, great gasping sobs, and moaned that she would do anything, *anything*, to get Frederick back, and she felt she was going to be ill, very ill, and *that's* why she was going away, because she *knew* she was going to be ill, and Frederick would have looked after her if *he* hadn't gone, and how could *anyone* expect anyone as old as her aunt to look after her?

I said *I* didn't expect it: that was her idea.

Then she told me what Frederick had called me, which was far from complimentary. 'And don't you dare say one single word against Frederick, ever; he was absolutely wonderful.'

After which there did not seem anything further to say, as far too much had been said already.

When, rather shakily, I tottered back to my flat, I found Mrs Aitch waiting for me on the step.

'Came back ter say I'm sorry I fergot Tom, but from the rumpus I gather you took 'im up?'

'Oh dear, was it as bad as that? Yes, I took him up, I mean I did take him up.'

Mrs Aitch said we'd better be careful as there was people

who didn't believe in living and let live, and minding their own business like she did.

I can't remember what I did with myself for the rest of the day. Probably I just sat it out.

4
The Cost of Living

AFTER THE BRISK EXCHANGE OF MISERIES AND recriminations, I did not see Alexandra again for months. For some weeks she was away, and when she returned she used to creep past my door, managing never to meet me either going or coming.

I felt quite lost without her. Not lost in the same way as when I had lost her to Frederick. But a deeper and reasonless sense of loss. She had just gone back to herself, and left me to myself. I saw her point.

It was nearly midnight, on a bank holiday, when she knocked softly on my door; knocked as she always used to do when it was late and she did not wish to disturb Mr What's-his-name on the first floor, although heaven knows he had had plenty to disturb him, what with scramblings backwards and forwards, and Frederick coming and going like the steps of doom, and Pisa getting herself so cleverly locked in the bathroom, and waving and calling, and Alexandra and I shouting uncontrollably at each other. But never a word, so far as I knew, had Mr What's-his-name uttered, either in protest or curiosity. He was evidently self-absorbed, which was an excellent thing for all concerned – especially for him.

When I opened the door, there was Alexandra, her light-brown hair wind-ruffled. She was wearing a stone-coloured dress, full-skirted, with enormous pockets, into which she had pushed her hands; she was playing the part of a belligerent young woman, ready to fly at me if I said a word out of place.

'Hallo!' She stared hard at me, daring me to comment on her sudden appearance at that time of night.

'Hallo,' I replied carefully, as though we had met yesterday. 'Would you like some tea?'

She relaxed a little. 'Yes, please. If it isn't too late. Or if you'd rather come up to me we can have coffee?'

We smiled at each other with a renewal of affection.

'It's like that again with you, is it?' I asked.

'Sort of,' she said; 'in fact, very.'

'Never mind,' I said. 'We'll totter through. Tea now, and I'll have coffee with you some other time. If that's all right?'

'Yes, please.' She sounded almost meek.

She followed me in, looking about her as though for signs of change. But there weren't any, except for the addition of one rather dim plant standing on the table in the hall.

'What's that?' she asked.

'A kind of vine,' I said, vaguely.

'How nice! Will it have bunches and bunches of beautiful little grapes, all sweet and pinkish?'

'No, I don't think so. It doesn't do anything. It's just a vine.'

'How silly! Why did you get it, then?'

'I didn't get it. It was given to me. By Marius and Bernhardt *ensemble*, believe it or not. But it wasn't a proper present, only an apology.'

'What for?'

'Well, they came together like a deputation, and they obviously had it in for me.' I hesitated, wondering whether the subject was still too sore a one for her.

'Oh, go on,' she said. 'Don't fumble around. It does no good.'

'They thought it was my fault about Frederick – at least about Pisa.'

'But they loathed Frederick, although they pretended not to.'

'So they may have done when you'd got him, but they were all for your having him when you hadn't got him.'

'How illogical,' she said. 'But then, what else can one expect?'

'I didn't expect that, I assure you.'

'I got what I didn't expect, either, so we'd better make the best of it. And you're a vine in hand, after all, even if it's the kind which doesn't justify its existence.'

'Would you like it?' I asked.

'No, on the whole, not, although it's noble of you. I'm too busy to give it my undivided attention.'

'Work?' I asked.

'Work? What is work? I'm living entirely on borrowed money. But I am livening up my background to start again.'

'Oh dear, to start *what* again?'

'Why, anything that comes along. One mustn't be static. So I'm painting the flat.'

'And how's it going, the painting?'

'The bathroom's blue streaks, the kitchen's yellow streaks, and the hall's what's called broken white with blobs. I bought one of those books which says it's easy if you know how. And

I read it all through, and now I *do* know how, but it still isn't easy. I haven't steeled myself to tackle any of the ceilings, but I'll have to, because they look dirtier than they did now that the rest is clean, even if streaky. I think the walls are wrong. They seem to be porous and just soak up the paint. It's a problem.'

'It must be,' I said with real feeling. I know what it is like to begin, and to be obliged to carry on, doggedly.

'And I ache all over,' she said. 'That's something the book didn't say. I think I shall write another called, *It isn't easy, even if you do know how*. But no one would buy it. The truth is seldom acceptable.'

By which time the kettle had boiled, and we sat around the kitchen table drinking our tea out of mugs, as we often used to do. 'It tastes good,' she said. 'Your tea's always much nicer than mine, and I never know why.'

'And so is your coffee nicer,' I said, gallantly and truthfully.

'Well, that's a pact,' she said. 'You drink coffee with me, and I'll drink tea with you.'

And we toasted each other silently. It was quite touching.

'I'm sorry that Marius and Bernhardt were so beastly about Pisa that they had to buy you that depressed-looking plant. It must have been awful.'

'It wasn't about that, really. I mean, it began as that, but we got on to other matters, and we got very heated and much affected, and we all shouted and banged on whatever piece of furniture was handiest. But it *was* awful. You're right there. I haven't properly recovered yet.'

'But what was it all about? I thought you got on so well.'

'So we did,' I said, and found that I could still suffer even at the recollection of the debacle. 'Especially Bernhardt and me. That's all finished, I fear. In fact, I know it is.'

'But what was it *about*?'

'Atomic energy,' I admitted, helplessly.

Alexandra laughed; I didn't blame her.

'How *could* it have been? You don't know anything about atomic energy.'

'Neither do they, and, of course, I don't. That's what I kept on telling them. But they went on and on, indefatigably. Obviously it was just an outlet. Having said all they could about you and me and Frederick and Pisa, they just had to find something else. And they did.'

'But surely you didn't have to let yourself be embroiled? Couldn't you explain that you didn't *know* anything about it?'

'You don't understand,' I said. 'That's what made the ghastly row. I kept on saying I knew nothing, and they got crosser and crosser and said that I must know what I'd read. But I don't read such things, because even if I did I wouldn't understand them, would I? Then they both rushed at me and talked at once, and said I was being purposefully obtuse, because I wouldn't accept what had already been proven by the best brains of the century, and so much more. They were both absolutely furious, and I still can't see why. Bernhardt said I was vain, because I thought I was above such world-shattering matters, and Marius said I was presumptuous, because I thought I was too grand to care. It was simply frightful and most unfair. All I was trying to do was to impress upon them how little I knew.'

'That's nearly fatal,' Alexandra said wisely. 'Men can't bear a woman to stand by her own ignorance. It makes them feel foolish.'

'And so they were,' I said, getting angry all over again at the recollection. 'What do *they* know about such things, when all is said and done?'

'Only what they read. And they're like sponges. They just soak it up and trickle it out, drip by drip, whenever the moment is propitious.'

'I hope I'm not at hand when the next moment is propitious,' I said. 'Anyway, I don't think I'll see either of them again. The fruitless vine was obviously a farewell. I don't know that I want to see either of them. They actually reduced me to tears, and that takes some doing nowadays.'

'Poor Marianne, I do feel for you. Isn't it a bore the way in which one's eyes let one down?'

I poured out some more tea. It was thin and weak, but comfortingly warm.

'And where have you been?' I asked.

'This evening? Why, to the Fair.' She sounded surprised, as though I ought to have guessed.

'Was it still going as late as this?'

'No, I went when it was all over. They were just packing up. The roundabouts still had their lights on, though the music had stopped. And the mess! Papers and cartons and straw and heaven knows what filth everywhere. People are disgusting. But the lights reflected in the pond, and the empty stalls, and the noises of everything being dismantled ready for packing, were worth it. Quite deserted, and terribly symbolic.'

'Oh, Alexandra, darling,' I said, 'you're not going to begin being symbolic, are you? That would be such a pity.'

'Only for tonight.' She smiled at me. 'I don't really go for that sort of thing, either . . . I saw an absolute pet of a policeman, very young and very tall and very good-looking, and he was making his way so disdainfully among the packers and the clearers-up. It was quite a pleasure to watch him.'

'Well, what happened?' I asked.

'That's just it,' she said sadly. 'Nothing. Absolutely nothing. I seem to have lost the common touch.'

'Never mind. You'll find another touch. A better one.'

'Do you think? Let's hope so.'

We drank to that, reflectively, in very weak, now tepid, tea.

'Talking of common touches,' she said. 'Donald wasn't one of my outstanding successes, was he?'

'He might have been worse. And, after all, he was only an experiment.'

'But he made me feel like *his* experiment, as no doubt I was. And he made me feel, too, that at least he was a good conductor, and I'm not really good at anything. Of course, he was right: but definitely lowering. And then he kept on talking about music in such inflexible terms. I always half-suspected he was talking nonsense, too, but I didn't know enough to take him up on it.'

'What's happened to Donald now?' I asked. He had swum out of my harbour.

'Oh, didn't you hear? He's going to make a new life for himself. I forget whether it's Canada or New Zealand, but it's somewhere with miles of sand and thousands of little white houses, all electric, and trouble-free, and all the time in the world to yourself, if you know what to do with it.'

'Donald will,' I said. 'He'll study a dozen subjects, and know absolutely everything about them. But he won't understand one, not really. And let that be a lesson to him – although it won't.'

'Yes, he was rather like that,' Alexandra said, and I was surprised to notice how soon Donald had slipped into the past tense.

'And now?' I asked, believing, rightly, that she would know what I meant.

'You're broke,' she said. 'And I'm desperately broke. But I thought if we could rake together just the minimum, the very, very least possible, we'd give a party. Not a grand party, but just enough to cheer us up. I don't quite know who'll come, but tomorrow I'll wander back and try to find the policeman, because although we got no further I think he knew I was attracted, and he wasn't exactly averse to the idea, and he *was* quite a poppet. He may be one of those quite special policemen, not an ordinary one at all, but just doing it to get his hand in, before he takes on some terribly important job.'

'He may be,' I admitted, but I could feel my limited enthusiasm draining from me. 'On the other hand, he may be a perfectly ordinary policeman, just as Donald was a perfectly ordinary bus conductor.'

'But Donald wasn't at all ordinary.' She sounded affronted.

'I don't think I know who is ordinary and who isn't,' I said. 'Anyway, what's Donald going to do wherever he's going?'

'It's some emigration scheme, and he's going to better himself. I expect he will too. And years later he'll come back to find us stewing in the same old pot, and he'll be no end lordly and full of helpful suggestions.'

'Then we mustn't be stewing in the same old pot,' I said, briskly, but without much real conviction.

'Oh, I know. But how one is hindered by this and that. For instance, there's Tom – a fat, undemanding cat, if ever there was one – just lying about and asking nothing. And what happens? Why, he isn't Tom at all, but Thomasina, and simply swollen with kittens. And now I shall have little blind mewing messing creatures all over the place, and have to pin notices everywhere offering kittens to nice kind homes. It's only a detail, but it all adds up.'

'I'll have one if you like.'

'Will you really? That's wonderful. I tried to book one up to Mummy. I thought it would be a comfort to her with old age creeping on, and all that. But Marius answered the phone and said Mummy was out being fitted for tropical suitings. She's off on some cruise. Marius sounded a bit stunned. And I've heard rumours that Mummy has a very flourishing new affair with someone quite twenty years younger. How *does* she do it?'

'Vitality,' I said, glumly. 'Just vitality.'

'Do you think we ought to take a course of something?' Alexandra asked.

'Perhaps, but what?'

Alexandra did not answer. We had another cigarette each.

'We'd save an awful lot if we gave up smoking,' I said.

'No, we shouldn't. I've tried that. We'd spend it on something else. You might as well say we'd save an awful lot if we gave up living.'

We seemed to have had that conversation before, too.

'You saw about Peter, I suppose?' Alexandra did not look at me, but carefully concentrated on the ashtray, by now disgustingly filled with stubs.

'No, what about Peter? I haven't seen anything.'

'Don't you take *The Times*?'

'What? At fourpence a copy?'

'The marriage is to take place soon. Perhaps it has taken place by now.'

'So he finally made it? Who's he marrying?'

'A young woman I've met once or twice at his parties.'

'What's she like?'

'Very reliable and most calm. She was taking a course in domestic science, and she had a firm grip of everything. No nonsense about Jung or Freud or behaviourists or getting oneself put right. If Peter feels he needs to be put right, she'll push him along to the old family doctor, who'll prescribe an iron tonic. It will all be very simple, and very good for him. I expect he'll sort himself out in no time because he'll get so sick of swilling down iron. And that's not vitality. It's sheer single-mindedness and never a glance behind. She isn't even specially attractive – not unless you're crazy about ponies.'

'Who'd have thought it?'

'In the future, whatever future there is,' Alexandra said firmly, '*I* shall think it and be first at the post. Nothing's impossible. I'd have said Peter would have chosen someone chic and ever so up-to-the-minute, and matching his car, but no, a perfectly ordinary young woman who knows her own mind. And he'll be perfectly ordinary in no time, too, and happy about it, no doubt.'

'Well, here's to them in tea,' I said.

We sipped and shuddered. It was cold and bitter.

'It's all turned out for the best,' Alexandra said. 'Peter's young woman isn't burdened by his confessions, and he isn't burdened by having confessed ... So let's forget about them now. And here's to us, and an end to this particularly beastly time, and never another.'

'And an end to tea-drinking,' I said.

'And coffee – except for choice.'

We sat silent and contemplative for a few seconds.

Then Alexandra shook herself free from the past, and became herself again.

'And now,' she said, 'for the party. There's Marius and Bernhardt – oh, don't worry, they'll come back to the fold, and be glad of the chance – and no Mummy because she'll be cruising with her latest – and a few of what you used to call the lesser Peters are still hanging around somewhere. Then there's the policeman – I'll go and do my stuff tomorrow, if that's his customary beat ... And I didn't tell you before because I felt so mad with you, but Mr What's-his-name on the first floor is quite personable, and obviously most equable because he doesn't seem to hold any of the kerfuffle against us.'

'Perhaps he's deaf,' I suggested.

'Now don't go and spoil it,' Alexandra said reproachfully. 'And if you should happen to meet anyone interesting between now and then, you *won't* forget, will you?'

I promised that I would not forget, although the possibility was remote. I never met anyone at all, except Mrs Aitch, to whom I still clung, although now that Pisa had gone Mrs Aitch should have been given her *congé*.

'I'll pay for Mrs Aitch to come in the morning after,' I said. 'I think I'm getting too old to face clearing up with equanimity.'

'Darling, that would be lovely ... I've decided, now that Tom isn't Tom, to do a proper book, very *mouvementé*, on his family, and you shall write it, and we'll make masses of money and give lots and lots of parties, and always have Mrs Aitch to clear up.'

Then we drank to that.

'Now, let's get down to it,' I said. 'What will it cost us? Putting it at the worst?'

'Let's do something a bit different,' Alexandra said. 'Let's do what they say in *Vogue*, or somewhere, and give a cheese party with masses of white wine. And make it an earlier one so that people arrive before they're quite worn out.'

'I've found a passably good imitation hock at five bob a time,' I said. 'Very dry and in the right-shaped bottles. No one would know, except the kind of people who do know, anyway.'

'That sounds perfect,' said Alexandra, chewing the end of a pencil. 'Let's say twelve bottles; that's – why, it's £3. Doesn't money flow! But we can't safely do it on less, can we? Then there's cheese, lots of different cheeses, and butter – about, what?'

'Thirty bob,' I said. 'At least. And cigarettes, say another thirty bob, or thereabouts. And extras and twiddly bits which one gets at the last minute. Say £8 – £4 each.'

'Um,' said Alexandra, and sighed. 'It isn't really any cheaper, is it? We could get quite a lot of gin for that, and lashings of tonic. And *Vogue*, or something, said one could give a cheese party for next to nothing.'

'Perhaps we're a bit nearer nothing than they are,' I said sadly.

'Well, why don't we get lots of gin instead and give a little late party, all roaring and merry?'

'No, I'm all for something different. Besides, I don't get merry on gin. It makes me weep.'

'I can weep without gin. I could now,' Alexandra said loftily.

'I'm sure you could, but that's not the point. You suggested cheese and white wine, and let's stick to that.'

'Oh, all right. £4 each, though. It still doesn't sound all that cheap, not to me.'

'Anyway, what's the party *for*? Why, actually, are we giving it?' Automatically I asked, although, I suppose, I knew.

'To meet some men.' Alexandra was impatient. 'The right kind of men. I saw dozens of men when I was milling around in the remnants of the fairground this evening. And you needn't look so sniffy, because someone who isn't *quite* might bring along just the person . . . And, anyway, it won't cost all that much. Not considering.'

Perhaps our addition was wrong. From what I remember it came to more than we had bargained for.

But then, everything does, doesn't it?

Also available in the Mermaid Collection

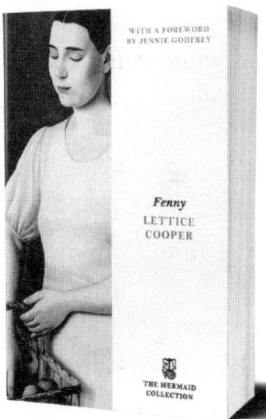

NURTURING WRITERS SINCE 1935

Also available in the Mermaid Collection

NURTURING WRITERS SINCE 1935